The Bedford Competition
Anthology 2022

Featuring stories by:

Juna Bine, David Butler, Claire Gleeson,
Anita Goodfellow, Juliet Hill, Andrew Kingston,
Judy Koot, John Langan, Eve Naden,
Jesse Perrin, Jean Ann Pollard,
Diana Powell, David Shelley Jones, Matt Thomas

**and
poems by:**

Linda Burnett, Lucy Crispin, Norman Goodwin,
Matt Hohner, G R Kramer, Scott Lilley,
Harry Lowery, Mary Mulholland,
Damen O'Brien, G H Plaag, Ricky Ray,
Laura Ross, Di Slaney, Lucia Wilde

ISBN: 978-1-8382586-7-2

OSTRICH BOOKS

...bury your head in a book.

Published in paperback by

OSTRICH BOOKS

...bury your head in a book.

www.ostrichbooks.co.uk

First published in Great Britain 2023

Typesetting by Elaine Sharples
Printing by IngramSpark

Foreword by the Chair of The Bedford Competition
Frank McMahon

It is once again a great pleasure to introduce this year's anthology of winning and shortlisted stories and poems and to offer my sincere thanks to all who made this possible. This year's competition judges have once again risen to the challenge of identifying worthy winners from 2000 impressive entries. Their dedication and skill in selecting the best stories and poems from so many talented and original writers is much admired and appreciated. Thanks also go to all our readers for their time and effort in helping in the initial stages of the judging process. It cannot be stressed enough that, without their support, the competition would not be able to achieve such high standards.

With entries from over forty countries, exceeding expectations, we have been able to make significant donations to our chosen charities for this year: Schoolreaders which assists pupils with their reading development, the Rothsay Education Centre which provides ongoing adult education opportunities, and CHUMS which provides mental health and emotional wellbeing support for children, young people and their families, as well as baby loss, and suicide bereavement services for adults.

It has been a great privilege to read this year's entries which give insight into the wealth of talent and ability from around the world. The many poems and stories in this anthology reflect the ingenuity and imagination of so many writers.

Finally, particular thanks to my colleagues Philip Carey, Marie Coles, Sarah Davies, Maureen Hanrahan, Rosalina Lionetti, Paul Moss, and Veronica Sims for all their challenging work. Thanks also to our many local supporters who have helped achieve another remarkable success.

Contents

2022 SHORT STORY COMPETITION

Short Story Competition Judge's Report
Tim Jarvis

'A genuine pleasure' is one of those stock phrases that has been emptied out of most of its meaning, but when I note it was a genuine pleasure this year to judge The Bedford Short Story Competition, I do mean just that. I read a lot of short fiction to whittle things down to a long list of forty stories, and then to a short list of twelve, and finally to select the three winners from among them. And I truly enjoyed all of it. The overall level was incredibly high, and all the stories on the long list were engaging and thought-provoking tales. But the final shortlist of twelve is a very special selection, any of which would make a fine addition to an anthology of contemporary short fiction. They cover the gamut from psychologically acute vignettes, smart slice-of-life storytelling, and engaging and believable tales of fishes-out-of-water, to harrowing drama, experimental storytelling, and eerie speculative weirdness. There is nothing stock or familiar about them, save when they deploy cliché to thoughtful, deliberate effect. And it was wonderful to see entries from all over the globe, exploring different cultural contexts, and displaying different approaches to the telling of stories.

All twelve stories on the shortlist are affecting, compelling works, and choosing winners from among them was an incredibly difficult task. But there were three among them that just had the edge due to the crafting of their powerful narratives. In third place is Jean Ann Pollard, from the USA, with *Bog Summer*. This is a powerfully vivid story, rich in descriptive detail, and as subtle and harrowing an account of young innocence defiled as I've read. *Chattels,* the second-place story, by Diana Powell from Wales, is a simple conceit executed brilliantly, with an innovative, almost supernatural point of view, and a powerful message. I was really compelled by the potency and clarity of the vision here, and the use of imagery, especially of the pond in which the young women look at their fresh beauty, about to be traded like so much horse flesh. And the winning story is *Six Foot Track* by David Shelley Jones from Australia. I was gripped by this powerful and original tale, with its compelling poetic prose, almost phantasmagoric crescendo as its rock star, lost in the wilderness begins to lose his mind, and its redemptive payoff.

Many congratulations to the winners, and to all on the short and long lists, which showcase the high calibre and incredible diversity of the art of the short story internationally today.

WINNER

Six Foot Track
David Shelley Jones

The track cuts through stunted trees on worn-down mountains, very old mountains of uncertain memory. They made it six feet wide so that pack horses could pass. Untended, the track has narrowed—so that now it's barely a track at all—sufficient, though, for a man and a dog. The dog tags along behind. He knows the dog is there, but when he turns around, there is nothing, only a hint of dog—a rustle in the undergrowth, a canine smell. Sometimes, to catch it out, he turns about abruptly—but always with the same result: no dog, just an impression of dog.

When he reaches a small stream, he stops and scoops the tannin water with a green enamel mug. The mug is a reminder of his scouting days. He was a bad scout. Unreliable, untidy, profane.

He drinks and splashes water on his face, knowing that this is the easy bit, that the plateau will soon give way to ragged, sandstone cliffs and he will be descending in a slipstream of crumbling rock. On unsure footing. Grabbing on to anything he can.

And the water in the stream will come undone, fall into the valley—a central, disorderly cascade—a halo of fine strands floating in the updraft. Like lover's hair. Like Cynthia's hair. He used to love the way she'd swing her hair loose on getting home, in their bedroom late at night, after a concert—back in the years of wonder when the band, his band, could do no wrong.

He sits for a while beside the stream, studying the fragments of sky that hang between eucalypts. He looks down at his boots, caked in mud. He looks to a far-off escarpment glowing yellow in the morning light. He cannot see the valley. It is country without middle distance.

He gets up and swings his pack to his shoulders and shouts *cooooeeee* and then stands still to listen. And all he hears is the hum of wind winding its way through the fractured landscape.

'Silly bastard. Silly bastard,' he mumbles to himself and presses onwards.

He's decided they've gone on ahead. Maybe they'll be thinking he's left without them. He knows they won't be happy. The fat banker will be saying he's a loser. Kelly will be discouraging them from hanging about because she has a boyfriend waiting at the other end. And the lovely guide? She'll be worried. It's obvious she's new from the way she reads from prepared notes, boring things like how banksia need fire to germinate and how everything was once completely underwater. He's sorry to be getting her into trouble.

When he's moving, he keeps his eyes squarely on the ground ahead. Because it can suddenly become wide-angle. Precipices appear without warning. It's possible to simply walk out into space. Into the blue.

He recalls the story of a German tourist who left his hotel for a bit of fresh air and a smoke. Who wasn't seen again until they found his body years later, on a ledge, close to the top of a nearby cliff. The surprising thing was that only one leg was broken. Apparently, everyone spent too much time searching the bottom of the valley. Which goes to show that pessimism rules.

He is haunted by the image of a rescue chopper and a stretchered, spinning man inching upwards to its jaws. 'Not me,' he says aloud; but he is uneasy—the red-checked shirt, the pants, the hair—a little hair has escaped the medivac shroud and blows about in the rotor wash. He imagines the man's face and sees his own: a grim rictus, an aquiline nose, full, rosy-red lips, an unshaved chin—rather square.

'Jesus Christ, not me!' He says a second time, pushing the image of the corpse out of his mind, trying to distract himself with thoughts of Cynthia. They should have worked it all out, stayed together, made babies; he should have cleaned up his act, gone to rehab. She was beautiful, perfect, brilliant, and now, even a little bit famous. He was an idiot.

He walks on in his red-checked shirt and baggy shorts and boots that should have been road-tested before the hike.

He is already talking to himself, and he's only been lost for two hours, which he thinks is reason to keep the pouch of dope safely tucked away. It's half empty, in any case. Some of it was smoked the night before while the guide read a book in her tent. He'd offered it around. Most of them had taken polite little drags—with the exception of Suresh. He had the tip of his joint glowing like a furnace, and he'd had to snatch it back. They'd all talked and laughed until, one by one, they retired. By midnight, only Kelly remained. They'd gone on to discuss cool things like the colour of mirrors and how long it would take to listen to every song on iTunes. He'd made a pass. She wasn't interested.

*

And now here he is, lost, looking like a total fool. Which, he has to admit, he is.

*

The next twenty-four hours are a blur, just puffs of memory passing like clouds. The emergence from bush. The brightness of sky curving over and around and down to the roof of trees far below. The valley waiting. He had once been told that wilderness is always waiting. By whom? He cannot remember.

There is a path on the valley floor that is barely a path, and he moves along it like a shadow, unused to the silence of soft ground, in a graveyard of fallen trees, with giant ferns blooming in the half-light, roots branching and sifting in the thick, black, worm-racked soil, flashing at him like pieces of bone.

This is the land before Adam and Eve, he says to himself, before dinosaurs even.

Occasionally, somewhere in the canopy, up in the dry, clear, thin white air, a whipbird whistles a long, drawn-out, middle C. Finding comfort in this sound, he responds by calling *cooooeee* again and again and again. Until he is hoarse.

Then he walks on, making arbitrary decisions on paths that fork and fork again; on looping paths that return to the beginning. On false

7

passages. In a world without reference to anything. Not to time. Not to place. No sun by day. No stars by night. He can't remember much about stars in any case, except that the Southern Cross is Southern.

*

Lunch on the first day was a Mars bar at the base of a boulder with an overhang.

Afternoon tea was a joint while sitting on a log at yet another fork in the track.

When the light grows thinner, he soothes himself by making plans, deciding that the evening meal will comprise of a Mars bar and a second joint. But he's soaked his matches. Late in the afternoon, at the base of a cliff, perhaps not far from where he started, he had heard the sound of falling water, like a distant rain shower. As he approached, the trees parted and he could see water tumbling down from a dizzy patch of blue in a perfect, even sheet. To strike a shelf of furrowed rock and make a fog of spray. To gather itself up and flow away. A neat little stream in a forest of shadows.

He found her there, veiled by falling water, Cynthia, naked and beckoning. He did his best to read her lips. Come to me, she seemed to say, come to me. Naturally, he'd marched straight in, without a moment's hesitation and lost his footing on rounded rocks. In freezing, knee-deep water. After righting himself, he'd got up and looked around and she was gone and there was nothing for it but to proceed onwards, wet and shivering, with the dog trailing.

The night, moonless black and fearfully cold, stopped him in his tracks and he slid down against a tree into a soft depression of fallen leaves. Using a torch, he selected the driest of his matches and struck the box—but it broke in two. He tried again with half a match and managed to make a little flame that quickly spluttered out. Please, Jesus, he said, before he tried a new match. This time a bright flame illuminated his cupping hands and he found himself in a cave of light like in a Flemish masterpiece, or in outer space, and he lit a joint. Feeling better, he reflected on his situation, noting that there was one serviceable match left. This match was going to be the fire match.

8

'They're sure as shit going to buy my music after I'm gone. I didn't give up the piano for nothing. All that practice for nothing!'

His teacher had cried when he broke the news to her, that he was giving up classical music and joining a band. She told him that she could take him to the very top. He will never forget it: the mole on her neck, the faint, downy hair on her chin, the tears rolling down her powdered cheeks. Then he got higher and felt great and he started to think about the good things. Cynthia. The girls. The parties. His family. Cynthia. It always came back to Cynthia. He smiled and shivered.

The joint became so short that he had to hold it in a delicate pincer grip between index finger and thumb, like a crab. That was the great thing about dope, he thought, the metaphors come thick and fast, the guitar riffs drop out of heaven. Of course, there is always the problem that inspiration in such circumstances comes in code. The punter has to be high to decipher it, so it isn't commercial. He recalled someone saying (and he wished he could recall who all these someones were) that if you drink enough absinthe, it becomes clear that van Gogh painted in straight lines. But you've got to drink lots of absinthe and not many people do. No wonder van Gogh died a pauper.

He considers the options while he smokes: let the joint go out, light another joint or start a fire. He lights another joint. And when it is nearly finished, he madly scratches about for leaves and twigs and attempts to start a fire with the still glowing tip, puffing at embers for all he is worth, failing and swearing. He tries to light a third match without result.

*

They came for him that night. They must have been waiting. The spirits floated in like unmoored boats, some familiar, some vaguely recognised, some unknown.

First came the spirit guide, floating between the ferns, gliding under the canopy of trees.

Then came Jeremy, the band's first drummer wanting his thirty dollars back.

'You don't need thirty bucks, mate, you're dead,' he said. And Jeremy told him that there was a girl over at the bar and that he wanted

9

to go down to the ferry wharf with her and a bottle of Jim Beam. Jeremy was always hard to refuse.

'So, there are girls in heaven?'

'Who said anything about heaven, I don't know where the fuck I am.'

'I'm sorry about letting you go, Jeremy.'

'That's okay, man. I can see the big picture now. I was too unreliable, wasn't I?'

'Yes, you were, Jeremy.'

'Was I any good, though? That's what I want to know.'

'You were pretty good. You could have been better.'

'The booze, the pills?'

'Yeah.'

'Did you love me though? Did you all love me?'

'We loved you, Jeremy. We felt terrible. You shouldn't have done it, mate.'

'I wouldn't do it now.'

'Jesus Christ, Jeremy, it's a bit late to say that!'

'I know.'

'If we could do it all again, we would have looked after you better. We were selfish arseholes back then.'

'It is what is.'

'Yeah, it is what is.'

And he fell asleep again and the cold crept up, its icy roots permeating every layer of clothing, burrowing inward towards his warmly beating heart.

Mrs Granger, the headmistress, with her hearing aid and Eau de Cologne, came next.

'You've got to get your act together, my boy, before it's too late. You could do great things you know.'

And then came Cynthia.

'We nearly had it all,' he said to her.

'We did have it all, baby,' she replied.

'Don't tell me you're dead.'

'I'm not dead, baby, I've just come to mess with your head. 'Cause you deserve it, you're a selfish bastard. You take more than you give.'

And, before he had a chance to apologise to Cynthia, she was gone.
And there were others.

Just before daybreak, there was a young man he didn't recognise.
The young man asked him:

'Do you remember December?'

He could not.

*

Sometime during the night, a tree fell. It must have been a very big tree.
It shook the ground and woke him up. He later remembered thinking: *I
am here for the tree, man, I'm here, that's what it's all about, being here.
Here not there.*

*

He wakes to the laugh of a kookaburra in the pale, grey light of dawn and
sets off, hungry and light-headed, to what he hopes is the western side of
the valley, measuring time with dry-mouthed, whispered songs,
navigating by the length of shadows. The dog follows, hanging off like a
mangy mongrel. He comes upon further crossroads as he knew he would.

The track ahead forks three ways, and he hasn't the faintest idea
which to choose. Despondent, he stops walking, convinced he is no
longer a lucky man, and sits on a log, filling in the time inspecting his
remaining matches, dropping them one by one into his upturned cap.
When he finds an almost dry match, he lights up and has a smoke while
the day grows brighter. Then Jesus comes along, white-robed and
bearded, walking towards him with gentle, even steps. He has a wooden
walking stick. He has kind eyes. He even has stigmata. There are needle
tracks on his wrists.

'Mate, am I glad to see you,' he says as he gets up, unconsciously
tucking in his shirt, taking off his cap, smoothing down his hair, aware
that 'mate' is too familiar a term for Jesus. If it really is Him.

He suggests a round of Texas hold 'em poker to break the ice,
knowing that Jesus is sure to win—although he has no money on him
and, probably not Jesus either, there being no shops in wilderness. But

11

Jesus declines and walks on down the track, gesturing to one of the three paths, before disappearing into the eternal gloaming of rainforest. Without even giving him the opportunity for a selfie.

He takes the path chosen by Jesus and emerges late in the day, in the car park of Jenolan Caves, half-running, half-rolling down a steep embankment until coming to a stop on bitumen between a tour bus and a campervan.

*

The rest was disappointing. No squark of two-way radios. No relieved search and rescue personnel. There was nothing for it but to cadge a lift to town. Where there was no office. Where there was no hiking company. Where no one knew his guide. He went to the car park behind the supermarket, to the space next to the stacked trolleys, and found it empty. The car wasn't worth much, in any case. The gears were shot. The wipers didn't work.

He found half a hamburger on a bus seat and shared it with the dog. He remained there until nightfall. Not a problem to anyone. Merely a derelict in a dirty, red-checked shirt asking himself if this is what it's like to be dead.

*

In the great chamber of Jenolan caves, amidst stalactites and stalagmites, the fog of breath lifts upwards in the frigid air. Whispered words are rippling, sliding along the limestone walls. It's night and winter and very cold. Like when he was lost. All those years ago. How many years? He doesn't know. Wandering souls lose track of time. Mountains have no memory.

Before him, his darling acolytes wait in eager anticipation. He is remarkably serene, given the circumstances, a moment that may never come again. Or maybe it will. Depending on unknown variables. But who cares? Who gives a shit? The dog has a juicy bone, and he is as ready as he will ever be; gym-toned ready, with hair grown long, the greying bits dyed black. Practised, polished to the nth degree.

12

He nods. The lights go off. The darkness is now total. Not even a phosphor smudge. Not even a retinal memory of light. Silence broken only by steady drops dripping down crystal cones, hanging for a bit, finding release, and falling into muddy little pools on the limestone floor. Counting out the aeons. Keeping perfect time. Always. Unlike Jeremy.

Then someone coughs. The lights come on again. With startling effect. To stun dilated pupils. To razzle-dazzle. And he is on the stage before them, the gathered, privileged few. With his organ, giant and rare, sitting sideways so that everyone can see. On a dais, hammered together three days earlier—each hammer blow a shock of sound.

He turns to smile. The audience is small. It had been a battle to get Parks and Wildlife to agree to anything at all. Humidity, they said. Humidity ruins the crystals. So only a small audience and a livestream to the world. Unavoidably, the ticket prices are high, very high, a million dollars a seat including champagne.

A humidity extractor hums, vermiculates, hovers like a giant silver worm above their heads, so that programs flutter upwards in rare flight.

A tuxedoed emcee says: 'Silence please.'

And he lives on in this before; before his fingers fly on ivory keys, before his feet dance, before the pipes sing.

SECOND PLACE

Chattels
Diana Powell

We are looking at the girl through the trees, as we like to do. Susannah, her name is. The daughter of Susannah, the woman with the face of a marsh-rotted turnip—but who knows how to work, that much must be said.

The younger Susannah has different thoughts, we can tell. Which is why we like to look at her.

Where she stands is in a glade among pines that bow heads and link arms, like schoolgirls keeping a secret close. But this is no 'tell-my-lover's name' game, nor stolen treat. What they hug is a mirrored pool, as clear as our gaze.

And now, Susannah unfastens her hair, unfettering it from the caps all girls must wear, because hair restrained in coarse linen is better for working. Better, too, for keeping the chiggers and punkies away, to stop them from itching and biting the delicate female scalp. So, yes, the cap is a good thing, in truth. But. Still.

We watch as the cap floats to the ground, and as she pulls her fingers through her tresses, to feel the air blow through the golden strands; gold as the corn we were told would grow here in plenty—which may be the case in some part of this vast continent, but not here, where we have found ourselves. No. Not here.

The cap floats, the hair floats, white, gold, catching the sun.

Our breath catches in on itself.

And then, and then… she loosens the ties of her dress. It, like the cap, falls to the ground, around her ankles. A spool of flax. She looks down at it gathered there, surprised, as if, maybe, she did not mean to do this. Yet *we* knew she would. All the girls who come here do the

15

same. Just as all the girls who come here wear nothing under their workaday shifts.

Susannah steps forward. She steps to the edge of the pool. And, like ourselves, like the craning trees, she looks.

We do not have mirrors, here. Yes, we brought them with us, packing them up in the old country, layer upon layer of hessian, bound with twine, to keep them safe. Only, they did not keep safe. Thrown into the hold of the vessel, crammed there with the chattels of a multitude of passengers, to be subject to the bucking of the boat on the long, long voyage. Roof-high Atlantic waves, storms, tempests. Then, those that survived, surrendered to the uncaring unloading of the care-less stevedores at the docks. And still our journey, their journey, was not over. Bundled, as we all were, into carts, to travel over miles of 'road'—that was not road, but some sort of mud river; or, if dry, pitted and crested, root-infested, all likely to shake the chassis of the most stalwart of wagons. That, and all its contents.

Then, if by one of God's miracles, a single cheval should find itself unscathed, to be lop-sided against the higgledy-piggledy log walls of our 'dwellings', God failed to further protect it from the hands of recalcitrant servants, or the weather He, in His beneficence, provided in this 'heavenly tract'—the rain and snow coming through the roof, the wind blowing through those same walls.

So…no mirrors here. Hence, the need for a calm, crystal pool, that reflects a perfect replica of all who stand at its side. And some might say that the Lord works in mysterious ways—that He has given us nature's perfection in the stead of foxed, warped images, trapped between frames of gilt or mahogany. Is that so bad?

And would those same souls say it is also God's work that so much other delicate cargo suffered the same calamitous fate? The young maidens who left the home country, fresh in face and body, for example. How many of those arrived intact at this Virgin Territory?

Susannah is one such. She knows it, as she looks down at her reflection in the pool. She sees it in her comely features, her shapely limbs, her flawless skin, her burgeoning breasts, that hair…She knows it, and is pleased at what she sees, for a smile plays around her lips. And soon, as if she wants to see more, she stretches her arms wide, and twirls

16

her body round, her head twisting behind, so that she can perceive all parts of herself. 'Yes, this is me,' she is thinking. 'And I am lovely.' And we think so, too.

Susannah starts to sing. A playful tune, to match the swaying of the branches, the nodding heads of the wildflowers, the winking of the sun. A tune to match what she is now doing, dancing? Her raised arms flounce and loop, while her hands brush the air. She lifts one foot, then the other. And her hips…her hips sway like those lithe boughs, as she thrusts one side forward, then the next, pirouetting all the while.

And we find ourselves humming along with Susannah, even though we cannot hear the sound she makes. For it is the same as we would sing when we used to come here. For yes, we used to come here for just the same reason as Susannah—to see ourselves in that pool. Thinking we would be unseen by others (except for those trees), thinking of it as a private place, somewhere to revel in our beauty and our bodies. As we were then. Before. Lucky, like Susannah, to have made it thus far, unscathed, unblemished, in all ways.

And that is why we watch Susannah, reminding us, as she does, of how we used to be. But are no longer.

Seeing her dancing reflection, Susannah's smile turns into a laugh.

Ah. A laugh. A long, rippling burst of merriment. A sound we barely recognise any more. There is so little to be happy about, there is so little time for laughter, with all the work we have to do, with the weather, with…everything. It is a pleasant sound; one we wish we could hear more of. Such is life, some would say.

Susannah has stopped her dancing, now, as she steps forward, ready for what is next. Her arms are stilled and lowered, poised to clutch herself, because she knows the water will be cold, even with the sun doing its best to rise above the topmost branches to warm it. Or peeping through, to look, in its turn.

And now she is in the water, little squeaks coming from her, to begin with, from the cold, but then, these turning to more laughter, as she splashes about, splashes herself. Splashes her face, those breasts, below her arms, between her legs, as if she is washing—which she is…another useful function of the pool. Laughing all the while. So much laughter that we laugh, too! We have not forgotten, after all! True, our breath gasps, and our mouths are unused to spreading in that way, for screaming requires different muscles. But, yes, we laugh in some fashion. Laugh, and laugh…until Susannah disappears beneath the surface entirely.

We are not alarmed. For this is what we did, wanting the water to lave all over us, ruffling our skin, before entering each and every crevice, cleansing; then lifting our feet off the bottom of the pool, so that we felt weightless, as we moved through it… seeing another world, forgetting the world we had left behind.

*

What alarms us is our thought. 'Don't come back up!' Mary and I both mouth together, then look at each other in dismay. Is that what we think? Is that what we would like to tell her if she could hear? Do we truly want her to end her life in this moment of happiness—caught in a shaft of sunlight, illuminating her in the deep, lost in a reverie of freedom and bliss?

Now. Today. Before tomorrow, when all will change.

Tomorrow is the day set for Susannah's wedding.

Susannah is to marry Mr Wilbur Fielding. Mr Fielding is older than the older Susannah and looks much the same. Susannah is to be Mr Fielding's third wife, the other two having died of hard work in all manner of weather. Of falling pregnant again and again, and giving birth without aid, being torn asunder; of grief from losing those children who survive womb and birthing. Lack of joy.

This is what happens here. An 'old' wife must be replaced, so that her work can be continued. Work in the house, the fields, the bedroom. For no matter how many children die, more must be procured. So that they can work, too.

Susannah, having only just arrived here, having recently been 'sent for' to join her parents, thinks this marriage is not such a bad thing. Mr Fielding, after all, has a good roof over his head, and owns a sizeable tract of fertile land, which is more than most who have settled here. More than her parents, whose 'home' is no more than a shack, that has already blown away twice since her arrival. And the land they own is swamp—hence her mother's looks, she is inclined to think, charitably.

18

Foolish Susannah. But we cannot blame or mock her for her folly, for we were the same. Like her, we thought such a match was to be welcomed, as we were welcomed, we believed, in our vanity, when the men came calling within weeks of our joining our families—the farmers, homesteaders, outbackers; widowers, all. Coveted for our youth and beauty, a perfect catch, an adornment for their desirable abodes; not understanding that the welcome was just as they gave to a new, strong horse or cow, good breeders all, or a wagon, even, fit, and ready to do service, in place of those that had failed.

True, I knew my proposed husband, Mr Lawrence, had been married three times before. And true, his previous wives had all died. But I, of course, thought I was different, and that it would be different for me.

And Mary's 'beau' had been widowed only the once—hasty re-marriage was a common enough occurrence in the Motherland, why should it be other, here? Yes, there was talk of his ways among the servants, but servants talk should never be heeded, should it?

'Should we tell Susannah?' That is what Mary and I have been thinking, ever since we heard news of this latest marriage.

Should we tell her *now*, for, of course, she rises from the pool (and yes, we must be glad of that, mustn't we?). And she will lie down, on the velvet sward of the clearing, to dry herself in the sun, before pulling her shift back on, and her cap, before heading back home to preparation and celebration, just as we did on our wedding eve.

Should we show her what has happened to us? Our hands…hands are the books of our lives it has been said. The story ours tell is not a pretty one. *Hard Work in a Cruel Clime* would be its title. The calloused cushions of flesh, the nails gnawed as a fretful child's, knuckles like the ends of a marrow bone, the skin, peeled bark from the oldest Oak in an English forest. Our hair—no need to capture it under a cap, anymore.

Our faces…. We are glad there are no mirrors, now.

Spines bent, ankles swollen, knees…so much to show!

And…should Mary show her back, the welts and bruises hidden there? For, indeed, the servants' talk was true.

'Do you think…?' Mary asks.

'It would be for the best,' I reply.

'For her sake,' we say together.

'Surely…'

'Yes?'

We are looking at the girl through the trees.

Lizzie her name is.

We are waiting for her to take off her hat and her dress, to look at her perfect self in the pool—as we know she will do.

As we have done. Before.

Mary, Susannah, and me.

THIRD PLACE

Bog Summer
Jean Ann Pollard

July.
Light like lemonade on the ash trees quivering against blue sky. Fragile blue. With clumps of cotton-candy clouds. One fatter, flatter than the others, seemed to be riding a current, like a tide in a sea high above.

'Rain,' my mother murmured.

'You think?' said one of my cousins, buried in a book.

We were sprawled on the porch of our big, grey house, fields all around, apple trees by the vegetable garden, pines and maples down the drive, while beyond us to the west where the sun was lowering itself, a beaver bog glistened in its glacial scoop. We could hear the brook purling in the dark as it tottered over boulders, dark because of lilac and honeysuckle bushes gone to riot.

My mother was sitting upright in a wicker chair fanning her face with the comics section of the Sunday newspaper. 'So hot,' she sighed, her apron starched, and a bowl of string beans in her lap waiting to be snapped. Cousins Fern and Maude were cutting costumes out of old, discarded curtains. 'Look, Aunt Flo. Look here, Aunt Flo.'

'Yes, dears.'

Scissors, spools of thread and buttons were strewn on the slick, grey-painted planking of the porch, and Ellen was crumpling patterns drawn on faded newspaper pages. We were going to produce a play out in the barn... although we didn't know the lines. Not yet: I hadn't written them.

'Get off the patterns, silly!' Maude complained.

'What patterns?' Ellen mumbled, who was slow.

21

'Oh dear! Now what...?'

'Don't worry,' Mother said. 'I'll draw some more. It's all right, Maude.'

She hated her name, my cousin did, because it belonged to Great Aunt Maude Hyacinth Louise who had married Great Uncle Charles Benjamin E. James, who had been nerve-gassed in the First World War before any of us were even imagined. She thought she had a right to be herself rather than someone's memory.

I agreed. I watched her cutting, oh! so carefully, glared at Ellen who had made a face but was crawling over to hold an end of the fabric, suggested that Ed and Joly might help a little...if they really wanted to be stars... and watched a Ruby Throated Hummingbird shoot past to thrust its thin, long beak into one of the opened Runner Bean flowers... thrusting at it over and over as if it couldn't get in far enough.

Ouch! I thought. *Does it hurt?*

My mother shifted.

'See its color!' Joly said.

'Iridescent!' Fern remarked.

'What's this play goin' to be about?' Ed murmured, dawdling on the bottom step.

'Dunno yet,' I replied.

The hummingbird shot past again, molested another blossom, made it quiver.

'Oh, how cute,' said Maude.

'You think?' said Joly.

'Here comes Nellie Sue,' said someone.

'Yes. Where's Ellis?' Mother asked.

*

It was summer. I was eleven. My cousins were with us once again because my parents were firm believers in sharing wholesome country living.

'Get them out of the sinful city,' my mother explained. 'Get them into trees and fields where they can learn something useful.' She was determined, my mother, and as she said, 'The cows are next door, and the horses, and the brook is here where the kids can swim, and the bog where they can fish, and the house is big enough, and strong enough, even if it's old.' And she never complained about all the extra sheets and towels and socks and underpants and shirts and shorts and cooking and cleaning and psychological counseling for occasional warring factions. So, seven of us, not to mention a neighbor or two, were noisily in residence.

'Where's Ellis?' she said again.

'Oh… in the bog,' I said. 'Caulking his boat, I think.'

'Fishing!' snorted Fern.

'Stuck in the mud!' said Maude.

'Well, he'd better come back soon,' Ed complained.

'Why?' said Joly.

'To set up the tent.'

'What for?'

'We're sleeping out, you nit, don't you remember?'

'Please mind your words,' said Mother.

'But he never listens, Aunt, and we've planned for days!'

'That's right,' she said.

'Ellis and Ed never tell me anything!' Joly whined.

'Oh, yes, we do!' Ed sputtered, 'You…'

But Mother spoke up calmly. 'Joly, you and Ed go get the bedding, and find the ground sheet, and pull down the big tent from the garage… not the little one, the big one…and cut some stakes and decide where you'd like to camp…probably down there in the pines…and, Ed, you use the hatchet, and Joly, you can have a cookout in the rock ring. And pack some brownies to snack on later.'

'Oh!' They set off eagerly.

Mother sighed again.

'But they'll get all the brownies!' Fern complained.

'And be quite busy while we girls make ice cream,' Mother said.

We grinned.

*

23

I was wearing loose white shorts made of cloth called 'sharkskin' which was popular just then…something tough and rather pebbly…and a light blue halter tied at the waist and neck, and leather sandals. With metal buckles. It was hot. I kept pushing my red-brown curls off my sticky face, trying to concentrate on lines and scenes and who would play what part and how many pennies we could charge my parents and an uncle or two and maybe some aunt; if they'd only arrive in time, and if Ed could really be the fox and Joly the boy who saves his little sister from… well… Fern could play a lamb…or maybe we should have a chicken chorus to make a racket…that would be fun…or maybe a wolf…Ellis would make a fine, bad wolf…so serious! All of it analogy, of course (was that the word?), analogy for human interaction. Someone, after all, had actually stolen our canoe, our sixteen-footer, just a week ago, which explained why Ellis was trying to build a boat.

'I think,' I said, 'I'll go down to the bog. Who wants to come?'

No one.

'Nellie Sue?'

'Not me.'

Mother looked at the clouds. 'I think,' she said, 'it won't rain after all. But don't be late.'

'I won't.'

I loved the bog. Loved the way the brook curled down the falls to wallow through it, loved the Joe-Pye-weed, the ivory Turtle Head, the spikes of sky-blue Pickerelweed, the yellow lilies; loved the beaver dam that backed the water up to form a pond, the way the Button Bushes swayed to dip themselves. I loved reflections. Loved the smell… of mud and frogs and snapping turtles and the lurking bass and…oooh…the eels!

Ellis had beached his boat part way up a beaver run. It was a box, hardly boat at all. Funny, really. But he was proud…even if it didn't float.

'How's it coming, Ellis?' I'd picked my way across the field, forced myself through mud and clumps of alders, and squatted on a big, flat stone.

'Good!' he said.

And I was glad. Mother'd said he was her sister's problem child "because his father never listened". Watchful eyes. Calluses on palms. Splinters. He was just fifteen, tall and thin. 'Like a rake,' Nellie Sue described it. Nellie Sue, my friend.

'Some boat,' I said poking at a sunfish. 'Think you'll finish it? Look! Look at the little ones! They shine like gold!'

He was leaning over my shoulder, 'Only when the sun hits,' tweaked the neck bow holding up my halter.

'Yuh.'

Shadows in the bog made snake shapes in the current.

'Think the fish would be afraid,' I said. 'Maybe they are… the little ones. They give me the willies, shadows like that.' (standing up) 'Time to come back and put up the tent, Ellis. Ed and Joly—' (smirking)— they'll put it upside down…if they can figure it out at all. Bottom on top.'

'Think so?' He'd moved away a little, placed a foot on the boat, and sort of hitched around.

'Yuh. Don't you?'

'I like to be on top.'

'What? Look! Oh, Ellis, look! The Perch are biting! See the circles? There! And there! Like golden wires! Crowns! Oh, look!'

I slipped a little, pointing, and he caught my hand, held on.

'Oh! Thanks—'

And then I saw it, something escaping from his swim trunks…*like a sausage!* held in check by clothing, half of it, working to get out, forcing. And then I saw his eyes and they were considering. He squeezed my fingers. Tight. And pulled. And I felt myself begin to float, like a baby sunfish, and watched as he pushed me at the hot, red, bulging thing that seemed to throb.

'For crying out loud!' I blurted, snatching away my hand, and leapt, not understanding anything because everything was new…although a curled-up claw had settled in my stomach. 'We'll be late!'

I did a mad hop past the boat, his legs, into the alders, up the muddy bank, began running for the field where it was light, wanting light, seeking sun, and…

*

Nellie Sue was saying, 'Your mother is some worried. Where you been? You know what time it is?' She was slapping mosquitoes with a fern. 'They ate at seven! Joly couldn't wait! Ellis said—'

And I must have made strange noises because she stopped, and slid further down the rocks where the falls began. Where I was washing. In the brook. Sitting in the place we called the bathtub where the stones had ground out hollows in the ledge.

'You hear me? What's the matter? What you doin'?'

I couldn't speak. Kept splashing, pouring water on my head, down my belly, sloshing up and down.

'Honey?' She was older than me, the minister's daughter from a church in the village. 'What's happened?'

I couldn't speak.

Eight o'clock, and the moon, like a silver grin, was slipping low into peach-colored ribbons over the pines. Glimpses of it twinkled when the ash leaves shivered: glitter falling into water, on her hair. She was wearing a sleeveless, cotton blouse and soft, full skirt, and somehow placed her sandals noiselessly on leaves, climbing down. 'Honey?' Holding out her hands.

Words wouldn't come. She touched me and I stood up slowly, plucking...I think she used that word much later...plucking at the light blue halter straggling down my back, one fist in my crotch, legs crossed.

'You...Where's your...Where are your shorts!'

I pulled my hand away so slowly, like a sunfish floating, and she saw the darkness on it, saw the wet. 'Oh, Jesus.'

I could feel it trickling, just a little, down one leg.

'Oh, Jesus help us now!'

But all I could see was the hummingbird poking at the fragile Runner Bean flowers over and over as if it couldn't get enough. And Ellis saying, 'If ya tell, I'll do it again!'

At the Stepwell
Anita Goodfellow

Jiera is here to see, but not to be seen.

At the stepwell the heat and noise of the city seem far away. When her mother was a child, this was the only source of water for the community and the women would descend hundreds of steps to fill their jugs. In those days the red sandstone shone, and the niches and pavilions were cool quiet retreats during the hot summers. Now the carvings are disfigured, the stone-stained grey by pollution and splattered with pigeon shit. It doesn't stop the tourists visiting though and there's talk of restoring the well to its former glory one day. It's a place she is familiar with as she comes here when she needs to escape her mother's vicious tongue.

Her father has gone to Jaipur to buy the wedding jewellery and she tries to ignore the doubts gnawing at her insides. She had heard the rumours in the market about Samir and the tourist.

Her mother tells her not to listen and says, 'It's just nerves, Jiera that's all. Pay no heed to what others say. Men sometimes misbehave before their wedding day.'

She knows it is wrong to spy on her future husband, but she needs to see for herself if the rumours are true. The water below reflects the orange sky, the shade of the sindoor Samir will paint on the parting of her hair at their wedding ceremony. She closes her eyes and thinks about being a married woman finally free from her mother's harsh criticism. When she opens them, the stepwell is quiet and the last of the visitors has gone. She knows she should be at home helping her mother prepare the street food for the market stall. She will pay for it later, although her mother's black moods have become less severe in the past few months as the wedding day approaches. Her and Samir's family have been close since long before Jiera was born. Her mother is his father's favourite cousin.

Then suddenly Samir is there. She draws back into the shadows as he peers at the water.

She is reminded of the day when he jumped in, the water splashing over the steps and her legs. She could only have been five years old, and she burst into tears, worried he had drowned. Her mother slapped her, but she didn't stop crying until Samir reappeared, his eyes twinkling with mischief. Her mother berated him for wetting the bottom of her sari and when she turned around to wring out the material, Samir stuck out his tongue at her back. From that moment Jiera loved him.

Samir moves down several steps before sitting, elbows resting on his knees. Should she call out? He hasn't even kissed her and now would be a chance. But then another woman appears, and she's reminded of why she is here. The woman is dressed in tight, faded jeans and a loose white shirt, the sleeves rolled up exposing her fair skin. A camera is slung around her neck—big and expensive looking. She creeps along the steps and crouches before clasping her hands over Samir's eyes. He stands, his laughter disturbing a pigeon. Jiera has never seen Samir smile in such a way before—it's like watching a stranger. He points at one of the pavilions and the woman angles the camera before taking some pictures.

Jiera waits for a few more moments before turning and going home.

She stops in the market at her favourite stall and does her best to smile at the stallholder who always slips her an extra handful of bhindi. A few stalls along she grabs an orange. When she gets home her mother asks her where she has been, but instead of answering she hands over the vegetables, and the stolen fruit. The lines around her mother's mouth almost soften into a smile.

*

Jiera grinds the ginger and cumin with vigour that evening and as she brings the pestle down on the fresh spices, she imagines she is smashing the tourist's pale face to a pulp.

The night is pierced by barks from street dogs and each time Jiera closes her eyes she sees Samir with the woman. It feels like there's a rock underneath her thin mattress as she tosses and turns. In the end, she gives up on sleep and quietly, so as not to wake her mother, feels her way to the rickety ladder and out onto the rooftop. In the street below a pig roots through some rubbish. The night air is cooling, but it does nothing to calm her mind. They sometimes drag their mattresses here when it is unbearably hot. It is hard to imagine leaving the home she has always known and going to live with Samir's family. If she stands on tiptoe, she can see Samir's house a few streets away where the slums begin—a white square a little bigger than her own. When she looks the other way the lights from the big houses blaze. Soon she will be Samir's wife and the tourist with her fancy camera will have gone. This thought warms her as she makes her way back to her mattress and sleep.

Her father returns from Jaipur the next day. She wants so much to see the jewellery he has bought, but her mother shoos her outside. She can hear them though, her mother's voice raised as she berates him for the poor quality of the gold.

They are meeting Samir and his family. Her mother clicks her tongue as she looks Jiera up and down. She shakes her head ever so slightly and adjusts her dupatta so her hair is hidden. They walk in a group to the gardens by the lake. She's worn her best sari with the silver thread, but if Samir notices how beautiful it is he doesn't say. One of the parents suggests Samir takes Jiera to see the flowers. The gardens are busy, and she wonders if the woman is amongst the crowds. She draws closer to Samir and as they walk, she studies his profile. He is taller than her by a head and his complexion is clear unlike her own, which is marked by the chicken pox she suffered as a child. She asks about his job as a porter. He tells her of the hotel and how grand it is. He says he sometimes gives tours to a few of the guests for some extra money. She wonders if that's what he was doing with the woman at the stepwell, but then she remembers the way they greeted each other. In a bid to be rid of the image she asks him more questions, which he answers in a flat voice. She knows she's talking too much, but she's proud that he has a job with prospects. A monkey jumps at them, baring its pink gums and sharp teeth and she cries out, reaching for Samir's arm.

He edges away, saying 'Let's go back and join the others.'

The day of the engagement arrives, and her sister comes to help with the preparations. Anya, seven years her senior, lives in the next village with her ageing husband and ever-growing family. Her mother places gold bangles on Jiera's wrist, which make a soft jingle as she moves.

As Anya applies henna to Jiera's hands she whispers, 'I envy you marrying Samir. He is so young and handsome.'

Jiera feels a frisson of satisfaction. She glances over her shoulder to make sure their mother is gone before saying, 'What's it like to be a wife?'

Her sister shrugs. 'Hard work.'

'But what about love?'

'Ah love.' Anya's lips form a tight line. 'You will find out soon enough. Now, hurry or we will be late.'

Both families are seated in the small room, but there is no sign of Samir. She swallows her disappointment.

'He's working,' Samir's father says as Jiera takes her seat. She knows that the groom doesn't have to be present at the engagement. The priest has already given his blessing, so this is merely a formality and another step on the route to womanhood.

Samir's family murmur their appreciation as they look at her, although his mother puts her hand around one of the bangles as if assessing its worth. She asks Jiera how she would go about making a dal dhokla and where she would get good ingredients at the best price. The questions keep coming.

Samir's father pats his wife's arm saying, 'If Jiera can cook as well as her mother, I'll be a happy man.'

Her mother waves aside the compliment, but her face is transformed into a smile so rare and fleeting it's gone before Jiera has registered it.

At the end of the evening the wedding date is fixed, and the families exchange gifts and sweets.

As the date approaches Jiera seeks Samir out, but he is never at home, so she waits outside the hotel for his shift to end. A tuk-tuk overflowing with laughing tourists swerves around her as Samir hurries from the hotel. He looks handsome in his black uniform. He's about to climb onto his moped when she calls his name.

He pauses. 'What are you doing here?'

'I wanted to talk to you.'

'Look, Jiera. I'm tired.' He gets on his moped. 'We will soon be married, and you'll be seeing a lot of me then. Now I must go and help my father.'

Samir starts the engine, waves and is gone, leaving her in a cloud of diesel fumes.

She can't face home and her mother so as usual she goes to the stepwell. She picks one of the covered pavilions with its carvings. From here she is hidden but has a view of the whole stepwell below. The stone elephants regard her with indifference. How many illicit meetings have they witnessed over the years?

Samir comes as she knew he would. He is still in his porter's uniform. So much for having to help his father. His lie brings tears to her eyes. This time he goes right to the water's edge. There is no setting sun today and the water looks dark and murky. He dips in his hand and dabs his neck. Once again, the woman appears, her fair hair cascading over her shoulders as she runs to meet him. They sit side by side, their fingers touching. When they leave, they climb the steps slowly, hand in hand. Jiera pulls back behind a pillar as they pass. In the shadows the woman giggles.

'Samir,' the woman whispers and then her words are lost as Samir kisses her.

Jiera holds her breath, her hands balled into fists.

'I'll see you tomorrow, Ella. Same time?'

'I'll be here waiting.'

And then they are gone.

Jiera walks down the steps towards the water and sits in the same spot. There's a hint of the woman's perfume, a sweet musky scent. The stone is still warm. The tears in her eyes distort her reflection. What if Samir calls off the marriage? Her mother will never recover from the loss of face and the gossip. Thoughts follow each other like a street dog chasing its tail. It comes to her then, what she needs to do.

*

The next evening Jiera makes her way to the hotel. Samir's moped is easy to find. She looks over her shoulder, but there's no one to see her take out the knife and slash the tyres. She hides the knife and hurries away.

31

At the stepwell Jiera waits. Children run after each other along the steps, berated by their mothers. Two old men are deep in conversation. At last, everyone has left and there are only the rats for company. A figure appears, head bowed. She walks a few steps before sitting. Ella. She remembers the sound of the foreign name on Samir's lips. Jiera creeps towards her, practising the words she wants to say.

'He's not coming.' Her voice echoes in the cavernous space.

Startled, the woman stands, brushing blonde hair from her face. Her eyes are a piercing green.

'Samir. He's not coming.'

The woman frowns.

'He couldn't face telling you the truth, so he sent me. He can't see you anymore.'

'And who are you?'

'I'm to be his wife.'

'I see. Do you have a name?'

'Jiera.'

'Well, Jiera he hasn't mentioned you at all.' The woman gives a little shrug. 'Besides, Samir has other plans. And so do I. I'm going to open a café. And Samir has promised to help me.' She smiles, her teeth white and even.

Jiera crosses her arms, but the rage is burning in her chest. 'We are to be married in a week's time. Our families have decided.'

'But that doesn't mean he loves you. Samir is a modern man. He's going to break with tradition. We love each other.'

Jiera unfolds her arms and steps closer. She slaps the self-satisfied smile. The strike must have caught Ella by surprise as she stumbles. She tries to regain her balance but then falls over and over, her head making a hollow sound as it hits each step. At last, her body is still, one hand dipping into the water, the camera scattered in pieces around her. She doesn't move.

It is dark by the time Samir arrives.

'I'm sorry I'm late. I had to walk...' His footsteps slow as he approaches. 'Ella.' As he calls out the woman's name, Jiera pulls her dupatta over her face and flees.

As she hurries away, she thinks of the woman's taunting words.

At Laxmi Nath Temple the cold truth of what she's done hits her. Outside the temple the street food vendors call out. The flower sellers join in, their baskets overflowing with orange, purple, yellow and white blooms. She stops and buys a garland of marigolds, slips off her flipflops and goes inside. Through a haze of incense, the Goddess Lakshmi regards her with black glassy eyes, her four arms reaching out. If Jiera worships Lakshmi sincerely, she will be blessed with fortune and success. As she places the flowers at the deity's feet, a calmness settles over her. At least Samir will be hers now. The aroma of peanut oil and cardamon drift inside the temple reminding Jiera that her mother will be wondering where she is.

Later, when her family is sleeping, Jiera opens the wooden chest where her wedding sari is kept and runs her hands across the blood-red silk.

*

The next morning, she decides to stay away from Samir in case he reads the guilt in her eyes. After all, they will soon be married.

*

It doesn't take long for word of the tourist's death to reach the stallholders in the market, and they talk of nothing else. At night, the police hammer on doors looking for information.

Her mother is stirring the mixture for the dal bati churma and Jiera is chopping onions when there's a knock at the door. It's one of the women from the market. Her mother goes outside and although Jiera can hear them whispering; she can't make out the words.

When her mother comes back her eyes are blazing with anger, but there's also something else—an expression Jiera has never seen before.

'I need to talk to you.'

Jiera stops chopping. She holds the knife—the same one she used to slash Samir's tyres.

'It's about that western girl from the hotel where Samir works.'

Surely her mother can hear her heart hammering. She fled the scene so quickly, what if she had left a clue behind?

33

'I'm sorry, Jiera.'

Her mother has never apologised before. The knife in her hand starts to shake.

'Samir has been arrested for the woman's murder.'

She realises then the expression in her mother's eyes isn't anger, but pity.

The knife drops to the floor and with it, her future.

Fish Knife
Juna Bine

I am old. I am tall as a wave and capped with seafoam. The girls are a turbulence around me. They are agitated crabs. Swirling sand. I am an aberration, but aberrations are common in this school by the ocean: Gulls flying silently through the cafeteria. Kelp blanketing the roof. Nets spilling out of all the lockers in one hall.

The girls form currents and eddies around me. They move in clusters, like sardines, for safety. I am invisible as water to them despite my sun-bleached shift, despite my hair coiling whitely in two gathered puffs, despite my fistfuls of fish, bundled at the tails, swinging from my two liver-spotted hands.

I feel sleek in my invisibility. It is a thing I have earned with age, and I treasure it. Shoals of girls in simple uniforms flood through the halls. I make my way through unerringly, cutting an elegant path. The fish in my hands thwap against each other. I leave a briny wake.

I head to the auditorium, where all provincial revelations must be made. It is stark. White. Thin cotton curtains are eternally drawn over meager windows. Salt air filters through. A low stage forms a promontory before the five meticulous rows of wooden chairs. The room is alert. Peeling walls pulse in anticipation. I step lightly into the low stage. My shoe hits the wood like a shell. Nobody has followed me into the auditorium. I savor the contours of my invisibility. It is heady. Soon it will break.

A scuffed table, riddled with arcane jokes and exuberances, perches demurely at the back of the stage. Shell, shell, shell go my shoes on the wood. I reach the table and lift my fish laden fists. Scaly flesh thumps sharply onto the surface. Gills gape next to pen-carved grooves. A scatter of jelly-shining eyes reflects marker glyphs of hearts, numbers, and exclamation points. I take a breath and lean my weight against the side of the table. It scratches against the floor in protest, as I maneuver it to the center of the stage. The old legs scree and gar until they settle complacently under the hanging lightbulb that acts as a spotlight for the auditorium.

I lift the hem of my shift to my hip and unsheathe a hair-thin knife which is bound to my thigh. It is so sharp that you would not know you were cut by it until the blade was drawn out and your blood blinked confusedly in the light. I place the knife on the table, perpendicular to the fish. I wipe my hands on my dress.

The light of the door is bisected by a woman so tall she grazes the lintel. Orla is mossy, she is oaky, she is silent as owl wings. Orla is sylvan in our world of endless sea. Once, I hated her.

I pick up the knife. Grab a fish by the tail. Slap it onto the table. I grab a gill, and pierce the chin of the fish, right below its unbelieving frown. My blade swims from chin to tail in one smooth stroke. Orla steps through the door. She is inscrutable as a fox. Her eyebrows do not move. Her steps are slow but unwavering, right to the center of the room. She sits down in the first row, in the center chair, and lifts her gaze. The skin around her eyes is smooth. Her lips tilt neither up nor down.

I dive my hand into the severed belly of the fish, and pull out a greenish black, tar-like mass. It oozes onto the wood of the table. I pick up another fish by the tail. Slap it down. Nestle the knife into the flesh. Arc from chin to tail.

'Mae,' Orla's voice is soft. 'Mae, this isn't right.'

I scoop another coagulated mass from the second fish and pile it on top of the first.

'There are ways to do these things. To talk about these things.' Below Orla's equanimity, something like concern swims. Something like annoyance. 'You don't just come into a school with rotting fish.'

I am methodical. I am unmoved. The scooped-out husks of fish are stacking higher. Their dark insides heap on the right side of the table, next to jagged, pen-carved letters spelling out 'KIRA & BEEZ'. Chin to tail. Chin to tail. The knife and I glide. We are unstoppable.

Orla crosses and uncrosses her legs. Her presence feels like dog hair stuck on the sole of my foot. I think of us when we were young, so many

36

lives ago. Running along the dunes, jumping over playful waves, shrieking with laughter like gulls. Her brilliant brown hair would stream behind her, glowing golden in the sun. My mind rang with her then. *Orla, Orla, Orla*, like the call of a plover. I think of our secret place, where a wind-gnarled cypress grasped for the siding of my uncle's shed, forming an inverted nest. I think of how we crouched against the wall and looked up at the numinous weave of sunlight and branches. We would make a net of our fingers and press our damp foreheads together. We were one. A single whelk in the shell of the world.

I think of Orla as she grew older, and I grab the tail of a fish. Orla as her lips grew fuller and she painted them red. Orla as she grew and grew towards the sky and the sun, towering over the other children in radiance. I slap the fish against the table. Orla, as she took a boy's hand and led him to our secret place. Orla, as she mocked me for knowing all the answers in class. Orla, as she stood outside my house and screamed after I dropped out of school. I pierce the soft skin of the fish, and arc. Chin to tail. Chin to tail. Orla taunting me on her way home from school, first as a student, then as a teacher. Orla looking away when she saw me bringing in the day's catch. Orla standing proud in the auditorium, explaining why development is good, why the hotel and the warehouses are good, how we are a community, how we will be rich, how we must always be on the lookout for opportunity. I scoop out the rotting innards. Orla not meeting my eye. My hand is stained by sickly guts. Orla absent. Orla not there as I stood and watched our cypress get wrenched from the soil, spilling viscera of humus and stone from frightened roots.

I will not look at her. I will not. I will not see the shadow of years between us. The shed torn down. The cypress uprooted. The seas of our laughter replaced by a motel-8 and a bed and breakfast franchise and a half-empty mall and endless pipes with their shocked brown slurries, vomiting complacently into our water, which spits back sick and stunted fish. Orla is speaking. Urging what seems to her like reason. I will let her words swim around me. I will not allow them to enter into my understanding. The knife is a ray. A skate. A sharp-finned wolf of the water. It moves with ease. Chin to tail. Chin to tail. I scoop. Sickly innards accrue.

If I look up, I will see Orla, and in Orla, I will see Corinne. Corrine, who came to town three days ago with clipboards and orange tape and unscuffed high heels which sank in the sand. Corinne, with her expansive gestures over the dunes, and her myopic visions of warehouses and manufacturing plants. Corinne, with dreams of bulldozers and level, unshifting ground. I watched her from my small boat, as her ringed fingers delineated my shore. Orla's words seemed to halo her movements. *We must always be on the lookout for opportunity.*

I will keep my eyes down. I will slice. Chin to tail. Chin to tail. I will pile the rotted brown guts on the side. I will be witnessed. Here is the rot of opportunity. Here is the stench of progress. I grab a fish. Hook my fingers under a gill. Cut. Dive my hand inside. Pull out the congealed innards. Look at all we have lost, say the brown guts. Do you see in this dark, stinking mass the absence of our dunes, our shorebirds, our clear water? I will be witnessed.

Orla talks, but I keep the meaning of her words at a remove. Let them whirl about my head. Let them be the soft murmur of waves at night. Her cadence is measured. Her gestures are slight and precise as a summer weasel. But I cannot help myself—the soft rustle of her voice is a balm. I will let it slide over me. I will not let the meanings in. Meaning is kept at bay through repetitive action. The blade enters. The blade slices. The hand plunges in. The rotted guts are removed. Fish husks hulk together on one side of the table. Piles of viscera on the other. The blade enters. The blade slices.

I am immersed, and it is a soft shock to look up and see the rows of moony, gaping faces before me. The girls fill the seats, stand between rows, crowd the doors, jostle, pull, and elbow each other in a hectic silence. They are profoundly animal within their stitched and folded clothes. Spit crusts the corners of mouths. Sweat stains shirts. Dirt makes crescent moons under fingernails. The girls are feral-eyed, hissing things.

They are eerily aligned. Here is a girl with sharp canines, smacking imprecations under her breath. Here is a girl with bony white fingers, grabbing her friend's wrist and shaking it. Here is a girl with scabby, scraggly knees, and legs like a stork, shifting her weight from foot to foot. Here and here and here, so even, so wild. Their limpid eyes, which opened first into salt-filled air, into dampness, into insistent wetness and seagrass-tuned wind, blink and dart, waiting.

There is nothing else to do. I cut. I scoop. I sort. The action is repetitive. It nests me within itself. I see myself through the eyes of the dead fish, and I seem a machine, a husked woman, a tide come on too fast. The girls' voices mix together until no words can be plucked from the horde. Orla's owl voice dots the susurration. She is calm, reasonable, insistent. She does not hear what is brewing in the room.

I cut. I scoop. I sort. It is soft and wet around the bones. Gelatinously flaky flesh accepts my fingers over and over. Always the same. Always the same. And then it is not. I swim my hand through the rotted guts, and something runs up against my fingernail. The something is thin, supple, and hard. I sharpen out of my reverie, and stare down into the ruined belly of the fish. There is a glowing, winking striation of gold, threading between bones, fingers, and blood.

I hold the gleaming thing above the cut, pelagic bodies. It drips dark viscera. Delicate loops link and link and link, forming a slackened oval which slinks across my fingers. A clasp in the shape of a bird holds it together. It is a tiny gold bracelet.

A warm and furious object thuds against me, and a small, dirt-crusted hand leaps from an unknown distance. Tiny fingers coil around the bracelet. The chain tugs through my grasp. The room roils as the girls snatch at the blood-slicked bracelet, swiping and scratching each other's smooth faces, wiry arms, and insistent fists. They are a storm given life. I am held below the screams, the tugs, the blows, the tears, and I cannot surface. I am held below the relentless pounding of the wave.

In the aftermath: scratches along the hall, cracked desks in the four small classrooms, shattered office doors, windows broken and glimmering like fresh snow, and one small circle of blood, gleaming and accusatory. For the rest of the day, the school is closed. A tension seems knotted above the roof of the building. Orla and I turn away from it and walk side by side, along the path to the ocean.

'Mae,' says Orla, and 'understand,' says Orla, and 'change,' says Orla, and there is something about balance, and opportunity, and needing to grow up. There is something about Corinne, and development, and about Orla being on my side. My side. If I just relent, just a little. Something, again, about opportunity. The breeze is smooth. It smells of gull droppings and rosemary. I don't respond. I feel thin in my stained dress. My body feels crumpled. Slack. The cotton drapes strangely over my bony shoulders. The fish knife in its leather sheath feels bulky against my thigh, despite its uncanny lightness.

We walk. Across the concrete, and the root-tightened dunes, and the wood planks, and the sand. Something tense has grown in Orla. Her accusations sound more and more like explanations. Like apologies. Our feet are old and thin in the slow tide. The sand sparkles black, then gold, and the traces of our movement are erased by water.

'Orla,' I say, and she tenses, half prey, half predator. Some slight motion flashes behind us. 'Orla, I tried—' Light darts through her eyes, and her brows arc strangely. The ocean pools its calm silk across our feet. Something is here. I am tense, and the moment expands. A whimbrel patters along the sea foam. A defeated blade of kelp lumps itself over in the breeze. My skin prickles. Orla's hand flutters almost imperceptibly. Her hair glows white in the sun. My gaze sprints over a rotted sneaker brought in by the tide, a burrowing clam, and a pipe, snaking to the hotel, spitting out a heartless soup.

Orla nods at the space behind my ear, and I turn. Corinne. Corinne, in her powder blue linen suit and impractical heels. Corinne with her sharp, immaculate nails curled around a monogrammed clipboard. Corinne gesturing above the dunes, pointing to where she wants to cut and tear the land, tracing vast angles in the air. *Imagine*, she tells us. *So much possibility.* Her smile is slack. Wry. No light reaches her eyes.

Unaccountably, the fish knife is in my hand. Time seems frightened by the blade. Moments hide and appear. Corinne's mouth gapes, unbelieving, and we are close enough that I can smell her cucumber-and-sardine breath. Her eyes are two trapped rabbits, darting with honest fear. My ragged, stained fingers are here, around the knife. The waveringly thin blade is here, below Corinne's chin. How did my hand find the knife? How did it leap, unwavering, to such violence?

The shed and the cypress come back to me like a vision. Like a ghost. Here are two damp foreheads pressing together. Here is clear water and wild laughter. Here are the endless dunes and the unimpeded sky. Something acrid and cold rises through my stomach, my ribs, my throat.

40

I find myself, through the wild leapings of moments, and it is as if I am seen from above. I note the knife, the pulsing vein in Corinne's tense throat, my shaking hand.

The blade finds no resistance. It is so thin that Corinne does not feel it pierce the skin, that she is confused to find it moving inside her, to see blood spooling into the shocked air. She does not understand how she can be on the ground. How the sand can be pooling red so quickly. How this pain blooms through her, faster than spring. Her frighted rabbit eyes skitter in disbelief, and then she is still.

Behind me, Orla. We are motionless, caryatids of horror. Her breath grooves into rhythm with mine. The air feels thick. Weighted. Then Orla shatters it with a harsh, guttural cry.

'Go. Go!' She wrenches the fish knife from my shaking hand. She is screaming, pushing me, standing between me and Corinne. 'Someone will be here soon, go!'

I am pushed back, and back. My feet trip on the sand, and I scuttle back like a crab. I cannot leave her here. 'Go!' Her eyes are unassailable. The look she used when we were young, when she told me, *We're going to learn how to do cartwheels this week. Steal me an orange. I am the mermaid queen, and you are my long-lost daughter.* I am pushed back and back by her voice, her arms, her burning eyes. I am running. Here are the dunes. Here is the endless break of the waves. Here is the languid sky. I run and I run, until I am out of reach. Until I am nearly out of sight. I stop. Breathe jaggedly. Turn to where a red stain glowers on the tawny sand. Two figures walk, then run across the beach, towards Orla, towards Corinne. Orla drops the knife. Puts her hands in the air. Walks slowly, calmly forward.

I Can't Hear You
Matt Thomas

'That one's my favourite. It was taken the day the school burned down. We were sent home and Jess's mother was cross. She called us skivers. That's Jess standing next to me, we could be twins, with our fringes and braces. You're in that one too—can you see, Walter, with that haircut that felt like sandpaper? Trying to reach something in your pocket. That day was the first time you noticed me.'

'They never found out who started the fire. Maybe nobody. In those days fires used to start on their own.'

'Everyone blamed Jess's cousin, the one who had to stay behind in junior school and hung around in the playground flicking his lighter. He had a scar where his hare lip was fixed.'

'Wasn't that Eddie Fraser, Molly? The boy who went missing?'

'I like this one as well. It's taken at the talent contest. It must be sixty years ago. Our eyes are popping, we're so excited.'

'And there's the boy, what was his name, who could make his dog bark. Didn't he win?'

'No, Celia won, don't you remember, Walter? She mimed to that song about going to her boyfriend's wedding. The faces she made; everyone was laughing.'

'I remember she pretended to sob and at the end she wrung the tears out of her handkerchief onto the stage.'

'The funny thing was she did come to our wedding.'

'There was a taste of smoke in the air for days. It made our eyes sting. We had to take the bus to a new school after that.'

'It wasn't really a school; it was a few prefabs no one was using. The rooms were so cold, we had to blow on our hands.'

'I'd written Molly on my hands in biro. I tucked them up my sleeves, I didn't want you to know.'

'Eddie Fraser wasn't on the bus that morning. I didn't think anything about it until Miss O'Donoghue asked when we'd last seen him.'

'He often wandered off. All the boys were in a secret club, but Eddie didn't join in with the rest of us.'

'Your voice is faint today, Walter. I can't hear you so well.'

*

'This one's special, we're on a school trip to the hat museum. That's Miss O'Donoghue with her arm round my shoulder.'

'Jimmy Eagles is pulling me away, he thought we shouldn't stand next to you girls.'

'Wasn't it Jimmy's dad that said he'd seen Mr McGowan talking to Eddie Fraser in the cut-through up to the war memorial the day he vanished?'

'Mr McGowan! He was the oldest person we knew. He was probably the age we are now, Molly.'

'There was a story he was a famous violinist, but he'd lost his nerve and given up playing. He lived next door, but he acted as if he didn't recognise us. He was like a hermit.'

'After a few days Jimmy Eagles' dad said he couldn't be sure it was Eddie he'd seen. Or Mr McGowan. My dad said it was a bit late to mention that.'

'Miss O'Donoghue always had her arm round me. I reminded her of someone, she used to say. Her sister, it might have been—the one who died of polio or scarlet fever. She let me look after the caterpillars.'

'I helped you feed them. I carried old cabbage leaves in my pocket.'

'Do you remember that day when we found them being eaten alive by maggots? All those white threads poking through their skin. Miss O'Donoghue said wasps must have laid their eggs inside them. I kept away from the wasps on the prefab windows. I thought, what if they do that to me?'

'You were so upset, we sat together on the bus home. Jimmy was giggling and nudging but I didn't care.'

'Jess thought I shouldn't be crying about dumb creatures. She said, 'Think about Eddie's mother.' They were still searching for him.'

'Jimmy's dad had a cruel streak, my dad said. He'd be all smiles, then he'd lash out at Jimmy for the way he looked at him.'

'People said he'd been shot at in the army and never got over the shock. But Mum knew him at school and said he was always trouble. On Friday nights you had to keep your distance, he could go off like a firework, Mum said.'

'Eddie's brother Ray got the blame for what happened with Mr McGowan, but it was Jimmy Eagles' dad that put him up to it.'

'We were all to blame.'

'We're still together, Molly.'

*

'Do you remember these, Walter? We took them at the farm. I'd borrowed Dad's new Polaroid. He loved gadgets.'

'I took that one. You're leaning against a pigsty.'

'I couldn't believe pigs were so huge.'

'Ray helped out at the farm, but they said he was cruel to the animals. Twisted their tails, I heard.'

'I never forgot that walk. The leaves were so green in the sunlight, they were like emeralds. I showed the photo to Dad. Beech trees, he said, they've been growing there for a hundred years. It felt like a message to us, to you and me. Make it last.'

'I can still picture the mud and our boots squelching through it.'

'And the old farm buildings that were falling to pieces.'

'When we reached the top of the hill, there was a reservoir we weren't supposed to go near. The police were there, looking for Eddie in the water.'

'I kept wondering how long it takes to drown, before you stop breathing.'

'One of the police recognised you. Told us to keep away.'

'It was Jess's brother. He was just a shy kid himself, Mum said. He was hungry. You found him some chewing gum in your pocket.'

'On the way back, we were walking past the farm, you said you were frightened.'

'It was getting dark.'

'You were shivering, I put my duffle coat on your shoulders.'

'This one is me with Mum and Dad and our old Morris Minor that Dad had to crank every morning to get it started.'

'You're all dressed up. Are you going somewhere?'

'There was a story in the Gazette about a new shop that sold everything. It had an escalator—we'd never seen one. Do you remember it, Walter?'

'It had automatic doors, like a spaceship.'

'We kept walking in and out to make them open. We didn't buy anything. It was just a day out.'

'My dad said what tipped Ray over the edge was the police coming to the door and his mum panicking when she saw the uniforms through the glass.'

'One of them was Jess's brother. He stumbled over what he was trying to say but from the look on his face, they all thought it was bad news. So when he said Eddie wasn't in the reservoir after all, it didn't sink in, they just went quiet. Then Ray started yelling and telling them to find Eddie before it was too late. You'd think he'd be relieved, but he couldn't take it anymore.'

'That was when Jimmy's dad said to Ray that he knew where to look next.'

'Mum heard the two of them bellowing outside Mr McGowan's house and we ran round to see what was happening. Mr McGowan came to the door and Ray pushed past him. There was all this clanging and crashing and swearing from inside. He was opening cupboards and looking under the bed for Eddie. When Ray came out, he shouted into Mr McGowan's face, something about him being crazy. Mr McGowan was shaking. That was why Mum helped him back inside.'

'My dad said no one had been in Mr McGowan's house for years.'

'I followed them in. The rooms were piled high with rubbish, there was torn-up newspaper and rotting food everywhere. The whole place was filthy and dark, and the stench was so bad I couldn't get my breath. Everything in the kitchen was covered in black slime, even the walls.'

'They moved him away after that, somewhere he'd be safe.'

'Mum was upset. She wondered how long he'd been living that way.

And how lonely he must have felt. She blamed herself but you can't always know what people's lives are like.'

'Everyone said Mr McGowan should have asked for help, but my dad said, maybe he did and we didn't hear him.'

'Mum said it was strange to think that if Eddie Fraser hadn't gone missing, Mr McGowan would have carried on living in squalor. He might have starved or died of cold.'

'Everything happens for a reason, my dad used to say. Hard to see what the reason is sometimes.'

'You sound a long way off, Walter.'

*

'It was Jess's idea to do this, to look at old photos. She knew what it meant to lose someone. It would be emotional, she said. Nostalgic, that was the word she used. When she said 'you', she meant me, Walter, but I meant us.'

'Your friend Jess was kind to me when I was first ill. I'd never seen inside a hospital.'

'I'd helped look after Jess's mother. She couldn't tell us apart at the end.'

'Wasn't it her brother, the policeman, that found Eddie?'

'We'd got off the bus and were waiting outside the prefab. Miss O'Donoghue was late—she was never late.'

'We were lined up at first but when no-one came to let us into the classrooms, Jimmy Eagles started running around and flicking me and the other boys with his scarf.'

'There was a lot of shrieking, and someone called out Eddie's name. I saw Miss O'Donoghue and she was crying. Her whole face was jerking.'

'The other teachers were laughing. I couldn't understand it.'

'Jess's brother had the idea of checking the old farm huts near the reservoir. Jess told him we'd been walking there, so in a way it was her idea too.'

'Eddie was upset after Ray made fun of his lip, my dad said. It wasn't the first time he'd run away.'

47

'Mum said he'd shut himself in the barn and the door was too heavy to open again.'

'He'd fallen and broken his ankle. At least, that's what I was told.'

'There was a rumour Ray had locked him in there.'

'Jimmy said it was so wet where he was lying, all his skin was wrinkled.'

'People made up so many stories about how Eddie got there.'

'Trying to make sense of what happened.'

'I often thought about how we must have walked past him. Mum kept asking, what if he'd never been found?'

'No one knew what the truth was in the end.'

'Every time I saw Eddie after that I thought about Mum's question: what if he'd vanished for good? I'd see him messing about on the school bus and I'd think about all the small things that happened in Eddie's life that wouldn't have happened if they'd discovered him too late.'

'I sat next to you on the bus.'

'And that all our lives are made of moments we can hardly remember and people we never see again. If we can hang on to them, we can keep hold of each other.'

'I wrote your name on my hand.'

'And now I think no one has really gone away, not really, not for ever, as long as we don't lose the stories of what they did and said and the lives they touched.'

'I gave you my coat to keep you warm.'

'You're very quiet again, Walter.'

'I'm still here.'

'Are you? Sometimes I can't tell.'

'Talk about the day of the fire, Molly.'

Most Likely
Claire Gleeson

We didn't call it a party to celebrate the murder trial of our old friend and classmate; that would have seemed crass. But that's what it was, all the same. A barbecue: a daytime thing, as they all were in those days, when the logistics of life with small children usually dashed any hopes of getting us all together in one place after dark. At least it was summer, and the garden big enough for the four older children to mess about without encroaching too much on our conversation. The baby, Rob's baby, slept almost the entire afternoon, so unobtrusive that several times I forgot he was there. Paddy had built a makeshift barrier around the grill to prevent anyone burning themselves, and if an inquisitive child did wander near one of the fathers would let out a roar that would send them scurrying back to the far end of the garden. Mostly the treehouse set-up down there kept them busy; not an actual treehouse, of course, there wasn't a decent-sized tree in the garden, but an elevated hut type of thing with a slide and swings attached, the whole lot done in a tasteful pressure-treated pine that we'd been promised would last ten years. Which it would want to, for the price of it.

'Celebrate' is the wrong word, anyway; really it felt more like a wake. All of us who had known Dominic gathered there together, with his absence—an absence that would be permanent, we were all starting to realise at this stage—the awkward seventh guest at the table. Nobody went so far as to raise a glass in his honour—it was really not like that however it sounds. It was just that need to be with other people who knew him, I suppose.

It had been my idea to get us all together that weekend, early in the summer. I think we were all in each other's heads much more than usual, in the run-up to the trial; before, we would have gone months without much more than the odd message between Lisa and myself, photos of the kids mainly, or some gripe about the lads. But now, suddenly, we were all of us back in almost daily touch, and it felt a bit like the old days. We'd started a new text group; the old one was still there, on my phone, the one with Dominic's name and photo in it, but we couldn't use that to talk about him, obviously, and booting him out of it would have seemed too—something. Judgemental, maybe, although God knows we were all doing a fair bit of judging. And of course, he wouldn't have had access to his phone, not at that stage, but still—it seemed too risky to chance.

Lisa and Killian arrived first, their kids—the same ages as our two, give or take—running ahead of them through the house and into the garden. I hugged Lisa, took the wine she was carrying, exclaimed over the dessert she had made, which put all my efforts in the shade. Allowing Lisa to lord it over me in all things domestic was an easy win; for her because she thought it mattered, for me because I knew it didn't, and felt privately superior about it.

We had all been friends a long time.

*

It had been about eighteen months since the news broke—the murder bad enough in itself, of course, but of no personal relevance to any of us beyond being Another Woman Killed. And then the mind-blowing shock of the release of Dominic's name, the photos of him being escorted into court to be charged. Lisa had sent me the link first, and I'd stared at the photo—Dom with his hand in front of his eyes, an unfamiliar stubble shading his face. I read the headline twice, peering into my phone like someone much older, trying to connect the two disparate things. Then the image disappeared as the phone rang.

'Lisa. What the fuck is this?'

'I can't believe it.' It sounded like she was crying. They'd had a thing for a while, back in college, herself and Dominic; and of course Lisa was always a crier, it never took much.

I was still a step behind.

'It says murder. They've charged him with *murder*?'

50

'I know. I know.' She sniffed; the sound grotesquely amplified over the phone.

'What—who is this woman?' I could hear even then the accusation in my voice, the wrongness of my tone. *This woman.*

'They were living together, I think. Killian says he'd heard Dom was living with a new girlfriend, but he didn't know anything about her.'

'What about Caroline? I thought he was still with Caroline.'

'No, that ended last year. So Killian says, anyway. He bumped into him in town one of the days, they went for a drink.'

'Jesus fucking Christ.' One of the kids was pulling at my leg, and I batted him away.

'What does Killian think?'

'God knows, he's swearing at the computer here.'

'I'll have to ring Paddy. He's going to have a stroke.'

The child was back, his cries more insistent; hunger, damp, need. I lifted him up, nuzzled his silken cheek.

'Here, listen, I have to go. I'll see you on Saturday, all right?'

That was the week of the christening of Lisa and Killian's youngest, and in the hotel afterwards, once everyone had got drinks and the cocktail sausages were being handed around, Lisa and I huddled at one end of the bar to clutch at each other.

'I don't, actually, believe it.'

We kept saying things like that; kept saying exactly that, in fact, staring at each other with wild eyes and bemused shakes of the head. What we didn't say, at any point, was *He couldn't have done it. There must be some mistake.* The thing was that we did actually, believe it. Not that we weren't shocked, of course we were, such an event could never not be shocking; it was just that, were you someone who had known Dominic for years, as we had, known him in all weathers and seasons, it was too easy to see how it could be true. When the initial disbelief had worn off, when it was clear that there was evidence against him, not one of us ever raised the possibility that he had been falsely accused, or that someone else had been involved. We just took it as a given that he had done it.

*

Rob and Hayley arrived slightly late; they had that harried, joyful look of new parents, all careful solicitation of each other. Rob carried the car seat like porcelain, setting it down carefully turned from the sun. Lisa and I took turns telling Hayley how wonderful she looked, for someone who had just had a baby; it was true, but I still worried we sounded insincere. Hayley was younger than the rest of us. She hadn't been at college with us—Rob met her through work—and none of us knew her very well.

I opened wine, and Paddy lifted stuff on and off the barbecue with stainless steel tongs, which he had ordered at ludicrous expense from some specialist culinary supplier, and which had been used exactly twice. I had spent the morning making salads from the Avoca cookbook, which had turned out fairly well, although not well enough to justify the effort it had taken. All that chopping. Neither of us were much use in the kitchen, but we liked the idea of being good hosts.

The talk didn't turn to Dominic; it just started there.

'Killian went into the trial, one of the days.' Lisa had clearly been dying to share this bit of news.

'*Did* you?!' I was staggered.

'Yeah.' A bit defensive, as he was about lots of things. 'Anyone can go in, like, they don't check who you are.'

I lifted a hand, palm outward. 'No no, I'm not—I wish I'd thought of it.' Although I knew I wouldn't have had the nerve.

'Did he see you?' Rob, who had had a bit of a hero worship thing for Dom, back in the day.

'No, I don't think so. I was up in the gallery, sort of behind him. He never really turned around.'

'How did he look?'

He shrugged. 'The same, really. I mean, all suited up, obviously, but—yeah, the same. He's lost a bit of weight, I think.'

I hadn't seen Dom myself in years; not through any falling out, it was nothing like that, but just the inevitable dropping away of old untethered friends as our lives revolved more and more around the kids and home. Paddy and the boys usually tried to meet up for a drink around Christmas, and again in the summer maybe, but Dominic was always an unreliable presence at these sessions, more often away in London or at his dad's place in Spain. He was a journalist, in a piecemeal sort of way; it was hard to see how he supported himself with the occasional bylines that would appear on my Twitter feed, most of them long, tortuous pieces for online journals and magazines with vaguely anti-establishment names. I would read them, most of the time, out of some ill-defined sense of duty, although the things he wrote about did not often seem applicable to the world I lived in now.

*

We fed the kids, on a big blanket spread out on the slightly scrubby lawn, and filled our own plates with burgers and sausages, and chicken that I prayed would not be pink in the middle. For a while the talk turned to other things. Rob and Hayley were trying to buy a house, an undertaking that was increasingly like a satire of itself; they now seemed resigned to moving way outside of what you could even generously call the greater Dublin area. I had a flash of guilt then, as I often did, looking at the house that we were halfway towards paying off, the garden that was generous by any definition. The truth was it had taken the death of Paddy's remaining parent to enable us to buy it—his father had died when he was very young— and still I complained daily about the pokey kitchen, the toilet that had to be gently coaxed into its flush.

Hayley got up when I started to clear the kids' plates, and helped to dole out the ice-creams, which could drip where they pleased in the patchy grass and the heat of the sun. Rob was holding the baby, high against his chest. It seemed funny, still, to see Rob with a baby; he had been in some ways the most resolutely single of us, the last to let go of what felt like freedom.

'How are you finding it? The baby, and everything.' I waved my hand expansively, trying to capture it all.

'It's fine.' Her smile was tired, whether of life or of the question, I wasn't sure. 'My mam's been a big help.'

'It gets easier.' I looked at my own two squatting on the picnic blanket, five and almost three, and wondered if this was really true. It got different, certainly.

I brought the plates into the kitchen, already a disaster zone to which I would abandon Paddy later, as I escaped upstairs with the kids. At the sink I filled a glass and drank deeply, staring out into the garden. I remembered other parties, other kitchens; Paddy's arms snaking around me from behind as someone—often Dominic—strummed a guitar in the corner. He had a voice, Dominic, a high sweet tenor that always came as a surprise. It was easy to see, in those moments, why women loved him so.

(Her body had been found wrapped in plastic bags in the shed. It had lain there undiscovered for 'a number of days', according to the Gardai.)

By the time I stepped back outside, twilight had fallen.

'Do you think they'll find him guilty?' Lisa was down to the last amber dregs of her wine, and I reached for the bottle to top her up. She looked upset, and I was trying to work out if it was genuine emotion, or the luxuriant thrill of our proximity to real horror. It was hard not to feel a bit of that. Nothing this interesting had ever happened to any of us before.

Paddy snorted. 'Of course they'll find him guilty. He fucking did it, didn't he?' Of all of us, Paddy was the one who seemed the most personally affronted by what Dominic had done. His sister Evelyn had gone out with Dom for a while, just after college; Paddy had pretended at the time to find this hugely objectionable but was clearly delighted. I had for a brief time harboured vague ideas of us all growing old together, the four of us bound by family gatherings and petty in-law resentments, but it had all fizzled out after a few months, and since then Dom had had a succession of women on his arm whenever we ran into each other. They were all of a type—very young and very thin, their long hair dyed some unnatural colour. They made me feel matronly, even before I had had children.

'You'd have to wonder, though.' Killian was starting to slur his words; he could be a messy drunk, sometimes.

'Wonder what?' Hayley's voice, coming out of the half-darkness.

'Well. You know what I mean. What she was like, what their relationship was like.' (*Significant facial injuries*, the reports had said, although those were not, apparently, the cause of death.)

'What difference would that make?' Her voice was too loud, and the baby at her breast startled briefly, his little hand flying out and up, before settling again to his furious suck.

'I'm only saying.' Killian shrugged, and I saw Lisa frown, and take a breath as if going to say something, and then not.

She was right, of course, Hayley, and brave too. I wanted to tell her that, I should have told her that—that she was right, and brave, and that we all knew it; that we weren't monsters, even Killian. It was just that Dominic had been our friend. But then two of the kids started fighting, and in the rush to separate and pacify, to gently admonish one's own child while assuring the other parent that theirs had done nothing wrong, the moment passed.

Things broke up soon after that. In the narrow hall we unhooked jackets and handbags, put shoes back on weary children, strapped the baby into his car seat, a buffer of foam and plastic that could not possibly hope to protect his butterfly skin, his eggshell bones. In the warm hugging crowd, I felt someone's hand stroke down my back and linger fleetingly on the seat of my jeans. Paddy was opening the door for Lisa whose youngest was asleep in her arms. I thought suddenly of the week ahead and felt exhausted.

The verdict came through just after four o'clock on the Tuesday. When I saw the news alert on my phone, the language typically brief and restrained, I texted Lisa.

So that's it. He'll be in for life.

Jesus. I still can't really believe it.

His poor mother.

God, I know.

And her family, obviously. The girl, I mean.

Yeah, of course.

Doesn't bear thinking about.

And saw *Lisa is typing* appear briefly on the screen, and then disappear again. Really, what else was there to say? I had a sudden impulse to cry, then, a hot surge that bubbled up inside me without warning, but I suppressed this; I was afraid it would look indulgent, appropriative even, although there was no one around to see. I felt, too, an instinct to text Paddy, a heart emoji or something like that, but as I began to thumb the keyboard it struck me that that seemed a bit too much like gratitude, for the sheer absence of anything like horror in our lives, and I resented the idea of having to be grateful for that. So instead, I put the phone away, and went back to the kids, and our quiet little day. Not grateful, but glad all the same.

The Oboe Player
Juliet Hill

How could it be that difficult? Your daughter decides to get married; you want to get her the best performers possible for the wedding reception and so you hire them. It wasn't as if he couldn't afford something pretty spectacular and he wanted to push the boat out. Major cliché of fathers and daughters but that's the way it was.

No, the problem wasn't the demand, it was the supply. He hadn't realised until he started looking just what an unusual request some things had become.

'An oboe player? Hologram, Deepfake?'

He wasn't even sure of the difference.

'A real oboe player, a person, you know a musician.'

'Or we've got a programme that sets you up with an instrument as if you were playing it: it doesn't just play the notes, it gets your fingers into the right place to fake it better, you know, so you really look like you're playing. Most people just want a keyboard or a guitar, but I suppose there might be an oboe version.'

'No, it has to be someone who plays. Really plays.'

The voice at the other end sounded dubious.

'You'll be lucky to get a fake one. What does it look like, a real oboe?'

He left his number without much hope and went to get a drink. Having tried online, he'd been hoping that a real person might have more local information or contacts. God knows why he thought that.

When they'd first discussed the wedding, he'd been surprised by Fiona's request.

'An oboe?'

'I want them to play that music from The Mission, the bit that Jeremy Irons plays.'

'Wasn't it John Malkovich?'

'Jeremy Irons was in the original. You saw the Choose-your-Lead version, you know, with Deepfake.'

'God, early Deepfake videos. I'd forgotten what they were like.'

'Yeah, it was pretty basic then. There was a sort of blur around the faces to hide the joins, and the voices never sounded quite right.'

'And the options you were given: do you remember random mashups like Gerard Depardieu as Maria von Trapp? Half the time nobody wanted to see the full video.'

Fiona laughed.

'Mum chose Danny DeVito in The Mission, just for a laugh. She said he was much better than she'd expected. I don't think she realised he'd never actually shot the film.'

They both fell silent for a moment. Then he picked up his mobile.

'I've got it, you can get home-holograms now. Why don't we get one of Jeremy Irons with a personalised wedding message? Maybe he could play the oboe as well. He's only been dead a few years so he should still be on the books.'

'It's not about it being Jeremy Irons. It's the music and the instrument. I've never heard it played live and nor has Andy and even if it's just the oboe without anything else, it would make my day.'

At least she'd said that about the other instruments. There was no way he was going to find a whole music group to play at the wedding but a solitary oboist, maybe elderly and retired, that was feasible.

He stopped by the Metropole to see what was coming up. Whitney Houston in Concert (again); Michael Jackson (ditto); Justin Bieber; Lady Gaga. All holograms now.

Musicals and plays were still using 'live' actors. He looked at one of the posters. A multi-cast version of Les Misérables with a choice of over 100 actors: *Make your choice up until five minutes before the performance starts and your headset will be programmed with the cast you've selected.* He'd only just got the hang of Deepfake video when Live Deepfake was developed. According to the blurb, this enabled creators to merge live performers with digitally captured footage (whatever that was) of well-known actors, in real time.

What that meant in practice was that the actors were working their arses off every night providing an onstage performance; more famous voices and faces, chosen by individual audience members were digitally merged with them; and the audience had to wear daft headsets to see the result.

He wondered what it would be like to be an actor in that type of tour. Pretty soul destroying probably. He'd accepted it as inevitable technological change, but Fiona and her friends hadn't been half as enthusiastic as he'd expected.

'Dad, it's all very well looking at the faces on stage, but you've got to think long term. On Sonia's course, there are fewer students every year, right?'

Sonia nodded.

'Our tutors don't know what to do with us now, you know, because it's all changed so much since they started. I mean, who's going to sing without autotune or voice compression? And on top of that, hardly any of us are going to work in TV or in theatre with our own voices or faces, so all the technique and character work they used to do is irrelevant. Well, maybe not completely irrelevant—I suppose some of it comes out in the performance—but we have no control over what the audience sees or hears. I guess it means nobody will care that I'm an Asian girl playing Joan of Arc, but you know, they were beginning not to care anyway.'

'Hasn't it always been difficult, as an actor?'

She gave him a 'here we go again' look.

'This is different. We were expecting it to change but technology was supposed to make things easier, to get rid of so many gatekeepers, you know? Soon they're not even going to bother with live actors in theatre. People are already getting bored with the same old names but they don't want unknowns so I don't see how it can survive as it is. It's a rubbish job now but at least it's work.'

He looked at the *Les Misérables* poster. At least these were established musical theatre performers, even if most of them had died. Maybe the celebrity craze had passed.

The Metropole box office had been closed for years but he went round the back of the building and the stage door was open. On the door there was a cartoon of the scarecrow from the *Wizard of Oz* in front of a computer screen with the words: *If I only had a Wi-Fi Connection.*

59

'Anyone here?'

'Hang on, there in a minute.'

The voice came from below and a few seconds later a janitor appeared from the basement, carrying a bucket and mop.

'Bloody cat threw up. You'd think with all these pissed actors they'd be the ones to make a mess, but no, it's the frigging cat. And guess who has to clear it up: the only bugger left in the building.'

His voice wasn't local, and he looked as if he was well past retirement age.

'Anyway, what can I do for you?'

'I'm looking for an oboe player.'

'An oboe player.'

He paused.

'Someone who plays the oboe. The musical instrument?'

'That's it. It's for my daughter's wedding and I thought maybe the theatre might have a list of local performers, you know, from when they did musicals with a live orchestra.'

'Blimey, that's going back even further than Deepfake. Real musicians?'

'I saw Hamilton here years ago, but I can't remember if there was a band.'

The man laughed.

'All programmed, mate. And they used hologram software to make the chorus look bigger. God knows when they last used an oboe player.'

He propped up the mop by the door and unlocked his office. Inside there was a tiny desk covered in papers, a key cupboard and a couple of video screens.

'Not glamorous, is it? I'll ask around, but all the management's done from Manchester now and those berks just book the tours. They've got a technical department with a load of algorithms to sort out anything else.'

'Here's my number. Eric Peters.'

He had no more success anywhere else, and he was just getting ready to tell Fiona of his failure when the man from the Metropole rang. He'd been cleaning up more cat vomit, described in great detail, when he'd come across some papers in the basement. Among the digs lists and contacts for freelance set builders there was a list of musicians.

'They're probably all about 100 now. Or dead.'

To his surprise Eric managed to contact a Spanish oboist who was available. Her name was Silvia and at their first meeting, he found it hard to believe that she was old enough to have studied before the music colleges abandoned instrumental teaching and switched to production techniques. Eric wanted to ask her about her musical career, but her expression didn't invite conversation.

At the wedding rehearsal she didn't play anything, just followed instructions as to where to stand and when to start and disappeared before he could ask her to join them for a drink.

The wedding and reception were held in a gazebo in the back garden, and everybody agreed that the weather was perfect, that the decoration was beautifully done, and that the idea of live music was a touch of genius. Few of the guests remembered The Mission and even fewer the music, but when Silvia started to play, it created an atmosphere that he could only describe as magical. OK, father of the bride cliché again, but it was true.

He looked around at the guests as they listened.

Some of the guests looked a little bemused as Silvia tuned up. Others looked at each other when she fluffed a couple of notes and the instrument emitted a strange squeak. Even Fiona frowned a couple of times when Silvia deviated from the version of the music she knew from the film.

But the children listened open-mouthed.

Silvia had agreed to play again at the reception and started to set up as they were finishing their dessert and coffee. Everybody commented again on the choice of music and how much they'd enjoyed hearing a real, acoustic musical instrument, though he couldn't help overhearing a few unguarded comments.

'God, not again. It's not exactly attractive, is it? She looks constipated.'

'Poor girl. She probably studied for years but now people want something a bit different. I had Princess Diana playing the bagpipes at my wedding.'

When Silvia started to play again, the music was more up-tempo and some of the younger children got up to dance. Their parents watched for a while before moving from table to table to chat.

It was only when Eric tapped on his glass to announce the speeches that anybody noticed the silence. The music had stopped, and the oboe player and all the children had gone. All eleven of them, most of them not yet teenagers.

At first everybody thought it was a game, part of the performance and they'd come back in with a surprise they'd rehearsed earlier. People waited a little longer, frowning now, until the whispering started in earnest and a wave of panic spread around the garden. The children really had gone.

Parents rushed up and down the street, shouting their children's names while simultaneously calling them on their mobiles. The police were called, and a team of officers started to search the house and surrounding area. One of the officers tried the oboist's mobile but it was switched off and he instigated a track.

Three hours later it was dark. The parents sat or paced around in the house, jumping at every inappropriate ringtone.

Eric sat with his face in his hands, quietly panicking. Should he have done a background check or consulted the sex offender's register? The parents had all been there with their children, but they would be looking for someone to blame. He should have got a hologram of bloody Jeremy Irons.

As the sun began to rise, the police started preparing to continue the search. Everybody had gathered around somebody's mobile to catch the latest radio report when a solitary bird was heard in the garden. Its song was picked up by another, then another, and then suddenly the full chorus, getting closer with each exchange. The atmosphere was immediately more positive.

But the sound from the garden wasn't the birds. It was the children. Nobody saw how or when, but they just appeared. The youngest were giggling and the older ones tried to explain but found it impossible to say where they'd been. Most of the time they refused to speak at all and whistled and warbled incessantly, which quickly took the edge off their parent's relief. But they were back.

A few days later, Eric knocked on the Metropole stage door and stuck his head through.

'Anyone home?'

'Bloody Wi-Fi. Hang on a minute.'

The stage door keeper looked up from his laptop.

'Oh, it's you. A little bird told me you had a spot of bother at the wedding, so I guess we know who to blame for all this racket.'

'I wanted to talk to you about the list you gave me.'

'Of course you do. I've already had the police here.'

'She was called Silvia, the oboe player.'

'That's what's got me foxed, mate. There was a Silvia here, years ago. She was in the band for *Les Mis*, and one night in the bar when we were all a bit pissed, she demonstrated a whistling language her grandparents had taught her. But I wasn't going to tell the police any of that.'

'Why not? It must have been her.'

'She's dead. Hung herself years ago. She'd just lost her job at a music college in Leeds and then the management decided to get rid of all the acoustic instruments in *Les Mis*, you know the story. She was found in the pit, the morning after the final show.'

He looked back at the screen and blinked.

'It was all hushed up by the theatre of course.'

'So, what are you saying? She was some sort of ghost?'

The man shrugged.

'Beats me mate. I reckon they've developed some new type of Deepfake thing, and it wasn't really her. I mean, those headsets we have to wear in the theatre: do we really need them or are they like the green glasses in *The Wizard of Oz*? How do we know anyone is who they say they are?'

'I don't know. Maybe…'

'And then there's all this bloody whistling. It looks like some teenage rebellion, you know, the kids finding their voices and so on, but what's really happening? The mobile and media people are in on the act now, aren't they? Stands to reason. Whistled messaging and suchlike and nobody over twenty-five or so can understand a word of it. That film was bang on, you know, the one with Michael York where they all got killed at 30. It's getting like you're finished after a certain age.'

Eric was glad to get back into the fresh air. Whatever had happened to Silvia, he couldn't see it was part of some evil plot. The world was much more random than that.

He sat down on a bench opposite a hoarding with a giant poster of a Beatles reunion tour. A teenage girl, maybe thirteen or fourteen was already there, tying her shoelaces. He watched her for a moment as she whistled to a friend he couldn't see and laughed at some shared joke. Something had changed.

And if Silvia hadn't been real, who was to say any of the missing children were?

But then the girl turned and smiled at him before running off. He shook his head at the absurdity of it all and started walking home with John Lennon's eyes burning into his back.

One Shot
David Butler

The pub was heaving with the rugby crowd. Above the din and jostling, Vikram suggested *Chez Max.* Pyotr guffawed: 'Yeah, *after* JJ's round!' JJ had a bit of a name. My funds were running low, but I'd no wish to head back to the flat. So, I told them I'd nip out to the nearest ATM. Behind Janine's back, Vikram made an obscene gesture.

It was dark outside, the neon dark of the city. It must've been raining to judge from the glare off the asphalt and the hiss of taxis. It felt cold after the fug inside. I shivered. I hadn't brought my jacket. Besides the usual smokers there were few about; no one at all at the ATM. No *queue.* There was a figure cocooned in a sleeping-bag. Hoody–face turned away. You don't normally notice these guys. But there was something about him that made me look twice. The hood was up, the head angled so that only a beard protruded. Something made me hunker down, all the same. Once I'd stowed the cash away.

His face was gaunt. And yellowed, even allowing for the street neon. The protuberant eyes refused to meet mine. A jolt took me, and I clicked my fingers: 'Donal Reid! For God's sake…' The eyes flitted onto mine, then rolled away as though having difficulty focusing. 'It's me. *Podge.*' I ran my palms over my baldness, as though to make a joke of the years. 'Paddy McHale.'

No response, not even a flicker. Temporarily, I doubted. I was cold in my shirtsleeves. There was, besides, a busy body footering at the ATM, watching. So, I ran through my wallet for anything smaller than a twenty, to gloss over the awkward situation. I located a fiver and held it out.

'You can keep your *fiver,*' he said.

*

65

I hadn't seen Donal Reid in twenty years. None of us had. He'd disappeared when I was in university. Left without a trace.

His name had come up the previous September at the school reunion, that was the size of it. There was a rumour that put him in Boston, another in a dosshouse in London. Someone had even heard he'd died. Any queries about Donnie tended to be directed toward me; for a couple of years in school, we'd been next to inseparable.

It had been one of those intense friendships between adolescents. He was a year older, painfully quiet, tall, bit of a loner. Except, that is, when it came to rugby. What he lacked in bulk he made up for in instinct. He was part of the team that was just pipped by Rock in the Senior Cup final. But he was never one for the repartee that's part and parcel of that sport and, inside Dublin's business fraternity, long outlives it. Donnie would far sooner slip away once a match was done. Only for that, he might well have captained the side.

I was bloody useless when it came to sports. I was pudgy, and to make up for it, a class joker. I was a good nine inches shorter than Donnie, so we must've struck classmates and teachers alike as quite the comical pairing. For two years though, as my late mother always put it, we'd lived in one another's pockets. What it was we found to talk about into or through the night, and with such intensity, I can scarcely imagine. If my reasoning could usually get the better of his, he burned with such sudden ardour that my common sense felt dull next to it.

The friendship burned out or fell away. I went to college, took a degree. He went to ground, to follow some vague dream of being a writer. He'd won some poetry contest or other, or he'd a contact who was a literary agent, or perhaps both. I'd be more confident of the details if it wasn't for a row that finished off the waning friendship. The occasion was my eighteenth; the location, the function room of the *Mont Clare* off Merrion Square.

I should've mentioned, Donnie was adopted. His foster parents were about two decades older than mine. An only child, too, which as my mother used to say, explained a lot. Perhaps that was why he could decide with so little compunction to abandon the nest. One way or another, he'd got it into his head that I should go with him. That was the import of his diatribe as he button-holed me, coming out of the jacks.

'What in God's name would I do in London? Solve maths theorems? With respect Donnie it's different for you.'

'With respect McHale you're talking shite. What you'd do is *live*! You're supposed to know about life at eighteen years of age? What I'm proposing, we take life by the scruff of the neck. At our age, Rimbaud had all his best work written.'

'Rimbaud,' I muttered. All I wished at that moment was that none of my new crowd would chance upon us.

'You're doing what, accounting?' I shrugged, yeah. 'At eighteen years of age, you've decided to spend your life to adding up other people's sums. Come off it, Podge! Is that what you were given life for?' He shook me, only half playful. 'One shot, remember?' His eyes were huge, and, I noticed, veined. One shot was the one thing he ever said on the rugby pitch, a rallying cry for his team-mates. They'd even nicknamed him One-shot.

At this point, a girl heading into the toilet threw me a sympathetic grimace. Most of my college friends thought Donal Reid faintly ludicrous. A few insisted he was a junkie. Yet something held me, like the wedding guest in the poem. 'What about your folks, Donnie?' He smirked. 'You *have* told them, right?'

'That's a cop-out!' He nodded, slowly. I could guess what was coming. 'Let me ask you something…'

'When I'm on my deathbed,' I supplied. It had been another of his catchcries.

'When you're on your deathbed and you look back on a life spent adding up figures, how are you going to feel? Proud of yourself? Ok. Suppose you make it. You get a house. Your kids go to Belvedere College. Is that all there is, *Podge*?'

'You tell me, *Don*.'

'I thought that I'd hang myself. Swear to God I would. What d'you say, Podge? Give it a year. If it doesn't work out, go back to your degree. Please!' Here he was actually tugging at my sleeve. 'Come with me.'

'Not everyone can be an idealist, Donnie.'

'That's bullshit. It's not about *being* anything. It's about *not* being a…a *coward*.'

I released my arm from his. 'My mother's not well.'

67

'Don't pass the buck! Jesus Christ, I'm asking you to…'

But I'd already begun upstairs.

'Fuck sake, Podge…'

I hurried through the doors. To my intense discomfort I'd realised he was crying.

Six months later he disappeared. It even made the newspapers. His shoes and parka had been found by Portobello Bridge, but no body was ever pulled from the canal. For several weeks his face looked out from photos pasted to lampposts and bus shelters. Over time these faded, like so many leaves. Why he'd left in so startling a manner I never learned. Perhaps he'd run up a debt or had got involved with someone. I only hoped that, from whatever garret he'd holed up in, he'd at least written his foster parents.

I told a lie just now. I said none of us had heard a word about him in twenty years. In fact, at the ten-year reunion, Mixer Murphy, the last of the Jesuits, had brought along a slim volume of poetry. A chapbook, published by an obscure London Press. *H,* by Donal Reid. It had been sent to the school: no letter, no note, not even signed. Mixer pressed it on me, insisted I take it. I let on to be delighted, leafed through it on the night bus, and never once thought of it afterwards. I never got poetry.

*

A few catcalls brought me back to the present. The office party was grouped outside the pub, variously gesticulating and whistling. Janine, with whom I'd had an ill-advised fling, began to approach, dangling my jacket from a finger. I immediately rose and took a few steps towards her. 'Who's your *pal?*' Her smirk, and her boozy breath, and the whole smug set of them filled me with sudden loathing. I tugged the jacket from her—she was letting on to resist—and turned away. 'Well fuck you,' she said. I listened to her heels clack away, then returned to the cowled figure. 'Come on Donal. I'll get you something to eat.'

It took a good ten minutes to cajole him. At first, he simply ignored my entreaties. Then for a while he got hostile. At last, he stood, teetered, said 'If it makes you feel better about yourself,' and shambled towards a fast food joint. Looking at the state of him, we'd little hope of getting in anywhere else.

The light was glaringly white, and under it, the ravages were shocking. His head was little more than a skull papered over with mottled skin. This was overwhelmingly yellow; yellowed, too, the globes of his eyes. The beard was a sad excuse, though it lent his mien something of the medieval ascetic. Worst of all was the ruin when he opened his mouth. Seeing my revulsion, he grinned. 'Methadone, baby. That's the smile she gives you.'

Mostly he sat in antagonistic silence. His manner of tearing at the kebab was ugly, deliberately so. He had considerable difficulty swallowing. He refused entirely to answer anything pertaining to his past. Neither would he talk about his foster parents, nor say whether they lived. At one point I noticed his habit of glancing at my wedding band, which I'd been twiddling. I covered it apologetically. 'You're married,' he stated rather than asked, mouth full. 'That her with your jacket?' For a second I was lost. Then I recalled Janine, her sardonic walk, her severe lipstick. 'God, no!' Was there mockery in his dirty eyes?

'Kids?'

I shook my head.

'*Happy*, are you?'

'Are *you*?' The retort was instant. I'd no great wish to think about Leanne, much less talk to this stranger about her. Time enough for all that. Then the kebab, half-eaten, dropped to the table and he dry-retched. I clocked the staff severely watching us. 'Hey,' I said, happily lighting on a topic as I helped him stand, 'I came across a book of yours. Mixer gave it to me. Mixer Murphy? Yeah, so he passed it on to me, oh a good ten years now it must be. Book of poetry it was.'

For the first time, something approximating interest animated his face. Something approaching the school friend of old. 'What did you think of it?' he squinted.

'God, Donnie, it's been a long time, you know?'

He snorted, tossed his head. At the door I let on I had to head off in the opposite direction. 'McHale, for Christ's sake lend me a hundred,' he said.

I'd fobbed him off with forty, muttering we were months behind on the mortgage. It was no lie, we were behind. I watched his figure lope off towards the canal. Then I began to drift in the direction of Spenser Dock. My steps were reluctant, my insides jittery. God alone knows what cocktail of thoughts, of emotions, of memories the encounter had churned up. I'd been a prey to mood swings of late, and that was a part of it, too.

I recalled what my father once said. For everyone that achieves their dream, there's ninety-nine *with real talent* who don't. The ninety-nine that spend their lives *not quite* making the cut: in golf; or in tennis. The ninety-nine that don't quite win the award or get the audition. All very well to be romantic about it, Podge. Remember, a paternal finger went up, biographies are only ever written about the one percent who made it.

He needn't have been concerned. I'd no great talent, nor ambition. He should have saved that sermon for Donal Reid. But no doubt *he'd* have replied (the young Donnie, the Donnie I'd hung around with, the Donnie who made the great plays on the rugby pitch) that at least the ninety-nine could rest easy on their deathbeds. They'd given it their all. You see Mr McHale, you've only the one shot at life.

Having no wish to entertain his '*Happy,* are you?', I wondered if I still had that poetry volume; whether, if I had, I could lay my hand on it. *H.* Like rugby posts. I had an urge to decipher the observations he'd collected ten years before, if that's what they were. Before he became a full-on junkie, if that's what he was. Methadone, baby. For the life of me I couldn't remember unpacking it after the move to Spenser Dock. Once or twice, in school, Donnie had shown me a poem he'd composed, but he'd always had to explain it.

By the time I got to the river my thoughts had returned to the flat. Leanne would be asleep or pretending to be. The marriage had long since cooled off. To be fair to her, she had taken her one shot. This was before we'd met. For several years after college she'd tried to knock a living out of interior design. These days, when she could get it, she worked in HR. Probably we'd have gone our separate ways, in another world. But we'd bought the place at the peak. Besides, if she were to finally decide on a kid, time was running against her.

Out of the blue, I was seized by the unfairness of it all. Why hadn't things worked out for her? When had my enthusiasm waned? After all, she was still a fine-looking woman. Ours was still an enviable address. I looked at the figure looking back from the merciless elevator mirror. Five foot eight, balding, thumbprints pushed under each sardonic eye. What if I could have seen *that character*, that night in the *Mont Clare*? Mother always said you play the hand you're dealt. But had I played it? Then I saw again the skeletal figure shambling away towards Baggot St Bridge. A single, slender volume seemed scant reward for a life thrown away.

Inside the flat I was more careful than usual. Solicitous. Leanne's bare shoulder was above the duvet. I folded my clothes onto a chair and drew myself in against her bed-warm body. I held her close, my face tickled by her hair. She muttered something. Then all at once I was sobbing, deep, painful sobs: for the world; for Leanne Kearney; for lost youth. For the way that enthusiasm, or love, evaporates.

I pulled closer, kissed the nape of her neck. 'You're drunk,' she said.

Pietersen in The Black Country
Andrew Kingston

The text was simple. Unequivocal.
'Dad. Please come home.'

Pietersen didn't have to check. The voicemail, too, would be from Hattie. He could dismiss the text, no problem, but maybe best to junk the voicemail. Otherwise, he'd run the risk of hearing it when he tried to make the bloody phone do what he wanted it to.

Pietersen was at an age when he found himself hemmed in by time-saving devices, which could pin him down and rout him out. Not so long ago, he could disappear. He could nip across the Atlantic and sidestep whatever university he was visiting, or gallery was exhibiting his work. The ability to melt away was something he'd embraced when his fame started ruffling and jangling and threatening to turn him into some kind of enfant terrible.

When things started misfiring with Eileen, these whimsical jags and adventures took a more embattled, more embittered tone. They became escapes, rather than explorations. Since the divorce and the kids had grown up? Well, Pietersen was more unsure about what the hell he was up to. He was running away, or escaping, but he was increasingly unsure about what he was escaping from, let alone where he was running to.

*

Mondays, Wednesdays, and Thursdays. Tuesdays and Fridays, he worked. He kept the weekend free for gallery and theatre trips. This trip's habit; this trip's order. A twenty-minute train ride, screeching away from New Street under black bridges and bobbing through stations thronged with people going home from work. Off at Wolverhampton to circumnavigate the corralled, blinking cranes blocking and surrounding the station.

The 'Black Country;' an all too appropriate name for an area steeped in filth, soot and forgotten, shallow coal pits.

The tarmac at the top of the lane running away from the city centre gave way as the land dipped under the railway bridge. Pietersen felt as if he was crossing a frontier.

Tonight, the cobbles were slippery. Drizzle hung in halos around the orange streetlights. Pietersen, over-dressed, felt himself slow cooking.

He ducked as he entered The Great Western and pitched, immediately, up against the bar. He caught the familiar smell he'd been told was hops, but suspected was just spilled drinks.

The bar server took her time to drag herself away from her gaggle of acquaintances. They were talking about an old colleague, same as last week. Lottie—is it 'Lottie'?—had pissed off her boyfriend by trying her hand at burlesque dancing, then had run off with a biker gang, somewhere on the south coast.

'Black Country Best?'

'Please.'

The bar server smiled and looked vaguely triumphant.

'It's off. Sorry. I can't change the barrel at the moment. I'm on my own. Can I get you something else?'

Pietersen took a different drink. "Something similar," he was told.

The server seemed to be trying her damnedest to get on his blacklist, but neither she, nor the pub were in the same league as some of his enemies. And besides, the list was losing its power. Pietersen didn't have the clout and was no longer relevant to people who, in the past, may have wanted to bring him down.

He walked round, away from the main room to the snug on the other side of the bar.

He felt blood flicker in his fingertips. An urge, but he persuaded himself not to listen to Hattie's voicemail.

A few more people came in. They were taller than the pub's usual crowd. Better dressed, too, and they spoke more clearly, with less of the local, whining, tail-away dialect.

A couple of these interlopers joined him in the snug. Their presence, and the framed memories of steam trains and teeming platforms made the room feel crowded.

Mondays hadn't been anything *like* this busy.

Pietersen rifled through his wallet. His rail ticket to Southampton was now two weeks out of date. He'd have to get in touch, at some point, to see if he could get the next boat back. He took his book out. Another couple, newly arrived, nodded across from the other side of the bar to his fellow drinkers in the snug. To Pietersen's relief, this new couple then went off in the other direction, into the main room.

Best or not, the beer was going down well. Pietersen blocked and immersed himself in his reading. He'd have time to sort his domestic affairs later. Perhaps a little sooner than he'd have preferred if Hattie made good on her threat, made a couple of days ago, of coming over and bringing him back home.

Would she? *Could* she? Surely not, but he couldn't entirely rule it out. Big and tough and uncompromising as Pietersen was, he had no defence against Hattie's will. She'd taken some steely determination from him, but most of it had come from Eileen.

*

The server emerged from behind the bar. There were three people in the snug now; the original couple had been joined by another person while Pietersen had been reading.

'Port and lemon, and two pints of Best.'

She put the tray down, and glanced towards, though not directly at Pietersen as she lifted the drinks onto the table.

The three other inhabitants in the snug looked healthy and friendly and, potentially, irritating. They all wore lapel badges emblazoned with the letters 'W.A.C.'

The man who'd arrived while Pietersen was reading was peering at him.

I should be used to this from the old days, Pietersen thought, but he could feel his palms sweating.

The newcomer cleared his throat and half got up before sitting back down again and leaning towards Pietersen.

Here we go, Pietersen thought.

'Excuse me? Gerard Pietersen?'

For a moment, Pietersen thought about denying it.

'I am. But keep it to yourself,' he said.

'I'm Trevor. Trevor Wash. My wife, Cissy. And Len. Bit of an artist himself, is our Len.'

Trevor turned, beamed at his companions and took a sip of wine.

Cissy and Len beamed back, firstly at Trevor, then at Pietersen.

'It'd be a shame if I did,' Trevor said. 'Keep it to myself, I mean. You see, we know you've got your retrospective at The Birmingham Museum, but we're running our own little exhibition. Nothing on the same scale of course.'

*

Christ, Pietersen thought. Fans. A tiresome part of the whole toxic machine. Not only fans, but middle-aged, well-meaning fans. The worst sort. Running their own self-effacing, self-deprecating exhibition, into the bargain.

'I hope it goes well,' Pietersen said. Too quickly? Did he sound dismissive? Oh well. 'A shame I won't be able to look it up. I've a train to catch, then an early morning start.'

Pietersen felt his phone jump and rattle. While someone—almost certainly Hattie—was trying to contact him, and while Trevor was holding court, he hadn't noticed Cissy reaching across the table.

Pietersen looked down as she held out her hand. She gave him a W.A.C. button badge, the letters bold, simple, and confident.

'That's us. The Wolverhampton Arts Club,' said Trevor. 'It would have been nice if you'd been able to stick around, but the members will understand.'

*

Pietersen felt the hairs on the back of his neck bristle as he unclasped and pinned the badge on his jacket lapel. Fans, people; whatever and whoever they were. Yes, they wanted a piece of him, just like everyone else did. Or used to. But they were giving, as well.

Pietersen realised though; in that moment, that he needed to push on and get out of England, pick up the beats and rhythms which made him tick and had propelled him into the public sphere; years ago. Since then, he'd been blunted by numerous private views, the not-quite-the-cheapest red wine in plastic and Styrofoam, the crap reviews—good and bad. And all the fuds, duds and mugs with elbows and ironic distance, packaging, commodifying. The hacks, the airport lounges, and the tired hotel lobbies…the filthy nine pm taxis, the tiresome lectures…

Trevor, Cissy, and Len were getting up.

'Wait,' Pietersen said. 'There are plenty of trains. It won't harm if I get in a little late. How close is your— '

'Oh, we're in The Brunel Room,' Trevor said. 'Here, in the pub. Out back, past the loos. Where the bands usually play.'

*

Strip lights buzzed the ceiling in The Brunel Room, while sporadically placed anglepoise lamps bizarrely fixed and taped onto canvas chairs shone towards the ceiling, reminding Pietersen of old footage of the London Blitz.

This, then, was where the bands usually played. The carpets reeked. Pietersen choked as if he'd walked into a chain-smoking, leaking wet dog. The contrast between The Brunel Room and The Birmingham Museum couldn't have been starker. Here, the artworks were a hodgepodge of styles, sizes and media.

'Well, here we are.' Trevor's face took on a strange, strained look. 'What do you think?'

Pietersen didn't know where to start.

'It's wonderful,' he said. 'Wonderful,' he repeated, as the truth sunk in. It was, really, actually, quite gloriously, wilfully and unexpectedly wonderful.

'Well look,' Trevor said, still looking abashed, 'we couldn't just *ignore* you, what with your retrospective down the road. I'm sad to say that some of the W.A.C.ers don't go into Birmingham. Ridiculous, I know.'

Trevor shuffled aside and waved at a couple of prints. A3 reproductions of Pietersen's most recognisable, vintage works, with lumps of Blu Tack visible in each corner.

'My God,' Petersen muttered.

'We couldn't keep the original size,' Trevor said, looking down at his shoes.

'No,' Pietersen said. 'Not to worry.'

The original pieces could be viewed in all their glory, half an hour away. These reductions removed the 'fuck-you' abstraction but gained something else—rather than demand awe and introspection, they looked at home next to a punk Risograph and collage.

Pietersen found another beer in his hand. He drifted and his feet sucked into the carpet. He felt the exhibition's pull, comfort, and energy, even before Trevor, Cissy and Len started admitting people with W.A.C. badges into the room. They were a polite, roiling group. Some gave him space and respect. Others smiled, and one particular couple looked to have been nominated; or had taken it upon themselves to welcome him to the W.A.C.

'We just wanted to say, Mr Pietersen, how much we admire and love your work. It's so exciting that you're here.'

The introductions and the crooked smiles. The landscapes, portraits, studies, and abstracts. Their brute deficiencies were obvious, but unabashed.

Pietersen felt an energy he'd not expected.

And he wanted to go home.

'Would you like to say a few words?' Trevor asked when the two met back at the doorway.

'Do you know? No. I won't. As an honorary W.A.C. member, I'm happy to stand by when you declare the event 'open.' If that's something you do. But do *I* want to say a few words? I wouldn't dare presume to.'

*

Trevor tried to order a taxi, but Pietersen was having none of it.

People had come through The Brunel Room. They'd smiled, laughed and been at ease with each other. Most importantly, they'd not so much consumed as gorged themselves on the artworks, taking in all the germs, ticks and tropes into the bargain.

Pietersen tried to remember the last time he'd felt so alive.

The sharp air outdoors hit him when he stepped outside the pub. A train clattered overhead.

'Dad, where are you?'

Pietersen gripped, terrified he'd drop his phone, or lose this fragile, transatlantic connection.

'Hattie? Darling?'

'Sorry, 'Darling?' *'Darling?'* Are you drunk, Dad?'

'Maybe a bit squiffy, honey. As they say, here in old England.'

'So, you're still there?'

Pietersen felt too tired, too impatient to answer her question.

'Yes, but tell me. What's going on?'

'Dad—'

'How's your sister?'

Pietersen listened to the customary litany of woe and disapproval, as another train rumbled overhead.

'She's still your sister though. Remember that.'

There was a pause. Pietersen let it play out, then drew a breath.

'Honey, could you check out flight times back to New York? It's about time I came home.'

Sacred Arrow
Judy Koot

A
ll it will take is one shot.
The doe wanders in between the snow-laden fir and pine trees. She appears white in the gray haze, a ghost in the lingering morning mist. She pauses. Looks straight at you. Her eyes are a luminous, iridescent blue that punches you straight in the gut.

For a heartbeat, your bow quivers. The mist droplets cling to your forehead like cold sweat. You cannot fail your tribe, your family—not now. But the deer's presence radiates through you, through everything around you, infuses the mountain woods with an unearthly vibrancy.

The doe doesn't move. Neither do you. You cannot look away. You melt into her lucid blues, bask in them. Something passes between you, something older than the ages. Despite your warm buckskins and furs, your body starts to tremble. You don't know what's happening to you, you just know you don't want it to end. It's the only thing in life that makes sense right now.

Something cracks.

The deer's head snaps to the right, yours too. In the distance, Little Wing is moving towards you in between the trees. *What on earth is your little brother doing here?!*

You sign quietly, motion him to stop. He freezes, and his eyes widen.

A *woosh* sounds behind you, a sigh. It swirls under your buckskins, and suddenly, all the energy drains out of you.

You don't have to turn around to know the deer is gone.

*

You shove Little Wing into the tipi; the heat slaps you in the face.

Elk, your sister, looks up wearily. She's breastfeeding your youngest niece by the crackling fire, sitting cross-legged on a bearskin, your other niece and nephew asleep next to her. The intermingling scents of burning wood, herbal smoke and animal hides say home to you like nothing else. Instinctively, your muscles relax. You don't like it, so you immediately knot them up again.

'I told you to keep him with you,' you say, with your back stick straight.

Elk's dark eyes flash. 'I'm not his mother!'

Your brother hides behind you, clinging onto you like a tick.

'And I'm not his father,' you say quietly, prying him from your legs, 'but we'll have to make do.'

Your sister presses her lips together, pokes the fire with a stick. You try not to look at her, at her emaciated breast, the protruding ribs. Instead, you focus on the children's winter clothes draped over the line, the heap of sleeping blankets and furs…Your gaze freezes on the stack a pace beside it: four neatly folded blankets, four wooden bowls on top. Things that will never be used again, not by Winding River and White Moon, your brother-in-law, and your oldest niece. Not by Cloud Feather and Wise One Above, your parents. Something turns over in your stomach. The baby starts to cry. Your niece and nephew stir. For a breath, you're surprised they're moving, they're still alive.

'Hush,' your sister coos, cradling her little one. 'Hush, my heart.'

She turns to her children who are now wide awake and chatter one over the other. 'Go back to sleep you two! *Now.* Ignore your uncle, you need your rest.'

She shoots you a look colder than ice.

You hate feeling like this, being treated like this.

You shove your brother forward.

'He ruined my kill.' As soon as the words are out, you regret it.

Your sister's head jerks up, her eyes are lightning. And now, they're all on your brother. 'You did what?!'

Little Wing whimpers and turns for the entrance, but you're blocking it.

Elk rises, stalks towards him, grabs him by the wrist. It's twig-thin, you're afraid she might break it. Break *him.* Still, you don't wait to see what happens next, get out of there like you're chased by a bear. Back

82

into the bitter cold, back into the worst winter of your life. But everything is better than being in there, where every little thing reminds you of all the things that were good once. Your eyes sting. You blink hard, tell yourself it's the biting cold.

You pull up your hood to protect yourself, to hide from the world.

Behind you, wails join the howling wind.

*

Your bones are aching from the many breaths spent crouching behind the Marker Tree. She doesn't show up. Neither do any of the other whitetails. When the first rays of sunlight peek over the mountain ridge and set the woods aglow, you follow her day-old tracks until you lose them at Wind Water.

'She must have crossed the ice.' Restless One, one of your older and more experienced hunting brothers, walks over to you and scans the frozen lake. 'The herd might be moving to the south.'

You shake your head. 'That can't be right. The last couple of nights—'

'I'm telling you, the signs are there.' He slips his kill bag from his shoulder and reaches into it. 'Look.'

The hind deer leg dangling from a leather strap in front of you is covered in blood and bite marks, the hip joint completely torn to shreds. That only means one thing.

'Where?' you ask.

'Found it at Winding Rock.'

'That far down?' That wasn't good. 'And you sure that's all that's left of it?'

Restless nods, looking grim. 'They took down three.'

'Three?!'

'Two does, one buck.'

He starts talking about the circumstances. His voice disappears into the background—you can't keep your eyes off the leg now dangling at his side. Normally, you hunters leave carcass remnants alone, but this is not a normal winter. You swallow, lick your lips.

Restless' eyebrows shoot up, pity pools in his eyes. He doesn't offer

83

you a strip of meat like he always does, doesn't take one himself either; he puts the leg back into his bag instead.

'If things get worse, we might have to kill the pack.' He sighs. 'I'd rather not, but they're closing in, and other packs might follow from the north too. Maybe we have to move south ourselves.'

'But that's Blood Tribe territory.' A wave of nausea runs through you. 'They never allow anyone…If they attack …'

'I know. But we have to consider—'

There's a howling in the distance, then another, a third and fourth. Fifth. Sixth…

You stop counting. Your heart races—you've never heard so many, so close. With a will of its own, your hand reaches for your bone knife.

'I'm telling you, the wolves are getting desperate.' Restless nudges you in the side. 'Come on, let's go.'

Together, you move through the woods in silence, checking your traps and looking for prey.

One by one, the traps turn up empty. Even those near Black Larch Meadow: they hold nothing, not even a snow rabbit.

'This winter won't last forever, you know,' Restless mutters.

He isn't talking to you—he's staring at the last empty trap, shoulders slumped, a look on his face you've never seen on him before.

*

That evening, you sit around the fire in the main tipi with the others. It's a small group, there are twenty-seven tribe members left in total. You try not to think of the moons ahead, you count your blessings instead: you are lucky today, luckier than yesterday. Today, there's soup with hind leg deer meat, crow meat, gray squirrel, and a few yams from the autumn harvest. It's not much, but it's something. And the aroma filling the space is the best thing you've ever smelled.

Surprisingly, the mood is cozy, almost festive, like it used to be. People are chatting and bantering. One of the elders starts telling a story about the time he met the Eagle God in the disguise of a beautiful woman, a story you've all heard one time too many. Restless is playing with your sister's kids while she's measuring and handing out the soup. Your stomach rumbles.

Your little brother wolfs everything down in no time. He sighs deeply, burps like thunder, and everybody laughs. He holds up his bowl, but your sister doesn't give him anymore. She's the Food Keeper until the upcoming full moon, a task everyone takes very seriously—a task that is sacred. But Little Wing is too young to understand that. He keeps on begging, whining.

'I'm hungry,' he says. 'My insides hurt.'

You can tell Elk is starting to get both desperate and annoyed. 'I said *no*. I told you, the rest is for the hunters, the pregnant and the elders tomorrow morning. You've had enough. Go play with the others.'

He doesn't listen and starts to cry. You pick him up before Elk will lose her patience and drop him down next to you. 'Now, you stay put,' you say. 'Remember what I told you? About the bear?'

He stops crying. 'He winter sleeps?'

'Yes. He winter sleeps. He remains very still, very quiet, very patient. He's the most patient of all the animals. You know why?'

'Because of strong?'

'Yes. He's saving up all his energy. So when spring comes, he will be big and strong, the strongest of them all.'

'I am strong!' He makes two fists and growls.

'You can be. Now you sit still and be a bear.'

'I am bear.'

It only works until you pick up your bowl and start finishing your soup. You saved the best for last: all the pieces of meat. Little Wing says nothing, but you hear him swallow next to you, and you feel his stares burning your bowl out of your hand.

You take a last bite and sigh, savoring the strong flavor, the tender texture.

'Fine, you win,' you say.

You put down your spoon and fish slivers of meat out of your soup, knowing you'll regret it later.

You feed him, and at the last bite, he nearly chomps your fingers off.

'Hey! Now you're not a bear, you're a mountain lion!'

He giggles and snuggles against your side. You wipe your hands on your pants, loosen his braid that has gone all wild, twigs sticking out of it. You try to tidy up his bird's nest and carefully comb his hair with your fingers. Before you can re-braid it, he drops back against your belly, asleep.

You snort and press him closer against you.

Little Wing stirs, clamps your arms. '*Do da,*' he mumbles, *father.*

You freeze. A surge of emotion runs through you, a pain so overwhelming you can hardly breathe. Everything around you disappears—you can't hear anything anymore, can't see anything.

When you're finally able to breathe again, Restless is kneeling in front of you: his hand on your shoulder, light like a feather—Little Wing still asleep in your arms, heavy, like a boulder.

'Are you all right?' Restless says softly. 'You want some larch tea?'

'I…' You shake your head. 'I'm fine.'

He releases his hand, stands up. Frowns down on you. 'I'll get you some anyway.'

When you look up, across the fire, your sister is crying.

*

You wait behind the East Marker Tree near Wind Water. The sun hasn't come up yet, the lake looks dark and desolate. The wind blowing across the ice starts creeping under your buckskins, seeping into your skin, bleeding into your bones. It's like you can't keep warm these days: you're shivering like an evil spirit is being driven out of you. But at least, the cold distracts you from the emptiness; the last few days you've been feeling so hollow it turned your body inside out, exposed your nerves, now all raw and in the open. Your heart is living outside of your chest, you're wearing your stomach on your belly—this early in the morning, it's already gnawing away at itself, and you're gnawing on a piece of White Weeping Tree bark. You hate the bitter taste and too much of it makes your gums bleed, but it helps against the nausea, the hunger. After a while, the darkness in your head lifts, the shivers dissipate, and the hollowness mellows. Somewhat. For some time.

She's back. You'd recognize her anywhere, even as a black shape against the deep gray-blue dawn. Moving, stepping, gliding across the ice, towards the edge of the lake. Towards you. She's not alone this time: in the distance, three other silhouettes are struggling across the ice, three of her herd. But halfway they halt, as if they sense you. She hasn't. Not yet.

You wait until she comes closer. The arrow shaft rests between your fingers, cold and smooth like lake ice, its feather tips graze your knuckles.

A couple of paces in front of you, she pauses, turns back to the others and bleats. Her call echoes against the surrounding mountains, and suddenly, the sun rises from behind the mountain ridge: the pink-yellow light slides across the trees, the ice, it drives away the gray-blue dark and sets the deer on fire. It takes your breath away. She seems gigantic, like she's expanding into her surroundings, her thick fur coat gleams golden in the morning light. *Maybe she is the Mountain Goddess in disguise.*

Your bow and arrow quiver. You try to realign, blink the sweat droplets from your eyes. You draw the bow. The doe's ears prick up; she moves her illuminated head, and now, she's staring straight at you. Again, those irises: still that otherworldly blue, still radiating something ancient. Still hitting you in the gut with their deep awareness and empathy. But this time you can't bear it, can't lose yourself in it. This time your gut growls, you can't help it. At the sound, her pupils dilate. You silently ask her to forgive you; and close your eyes.

Stargazing
John Langan

We didn't notice the stars when we set out. The yellow haze of the streetlamps seemed to hide them, so you might easily think that the sky was altogether without stars, and the streets we walked in were the only possible world.

Moggy had brought a rotten egg with him: it was warming in his jacket pocket like a little bomb. Tonight, was *Mischief Night;* so the fourth of November was known round our way—a kind of local feast of misrule and licence. We were fifteen, and things like exams and jobs—the whole dreary business of becoming a pale, productive citizen—lay before us. So perhaps we needed our little dream of anarchy.

'We shoulda brought bangers. It's better wi' bangers. Tha puts banger in a little bag wi' egg, lights it, shoves it through letter box and then—*splat*! Raight laff!'

Rabbit looked doubtful. Hunched in his parka, he seemed distant and reticent, as though he didn't really want to be around. This wasn't his night and, when I recall it now, it's Moggy whom I see most clearly.

'Ah can tell tha dun't approve, Rabbit. Tha so law-abidin', so respectable! What's tha want ter be respectable for? What's in it fer likes o' thee and me?'

'Just don't want ter get nicked, that's all. Tha bound ter get nicked. Somebody'll see thi— it's not worth it!'

'Come on, Rabbit—owt's worth doin' once. Tha's only one life!'

The spirit of Mischief Night—or rather some spirit of his own creation or invocation—had possessed Moggy. Maybe it was just because he knew that he'd soon be working, or perhaps (if he was lucky) studying at the sixth-form college or the tech, so he had this one opportunity to do whatever you were supposed to do on Mischief Night. He didn't want to go to the grave of adulthood without tasting all the freedoms of the lawless lad.

I'd have been content to go round to his house—his parents were out for the evening—with a few bottles of cider; bought from some off-licence rash enough to serve us, and listen to Moggy's records, by obscure bands nobody else had ever heard of. And perhaps to look at the stars and planets through the telescope he kept in his poky bedroom, trained on the narrow band of sky you could see above the neighbours' houses and beyond the glare of the town.

It wasn't safe to look too clever or studious hereabouts, but Moggy was almost religiously fascinated by the night sky, by its limitless possibilities, and didn't care to conceal his passion for astronomy. His father had got him the telescope, second-hand, after he'd come top of the year in the end of fourth-form physics exam. Through it, he'd shown me Jupiter, Venus, Mars, and Saturn. He seemed to know exactly where to look and could identify things which, to me, remained mysterious and unnameable.

'Why don't we get some cider and just go back ter tha' 'ouse? Thi parents aren't in. Ah'll ask fer cider, if tha dun't want to'

'Ah can get served as easy as tha can! Any road, what's matter wi' thi? Tha're as bad as Rabbit! Tha's no spark!'

'But if tha's no bangers Moggy, what does tha think tha can do wi' egg?'

'Tha dun't necessarily need bangers. Tha just finds someone's car, some posh car just cleaned-'

'Posh car— rahnd 'ere! 'Oo's gorra fuckin' posh car rahnd 'ere?'

Rabbit and I laughed sardonically—sometimes Moggy's imagination got the better of him. He'd set an impossible aspiration for himself here, surely: an ideal of mischief, which couldn't be realized—or at least, not as he'd imagined it.

We'd walked down the hill from Rabbit's house into the estate. Blocks of low-rise council flats, interspersed with terraces of small houses, lined each side of the road, which snaked gradually downwards. In the valley floor were the steelworks. You would often hear the steel hammers pounding away in those days, like the great footsteps of an angry deity. The industrial smell too was very distinct—chemical, pungent, almost sewage-like. People would joke—people from outside the town, that is— that you could smell the place as you passed by on the motorway.

'All right for thee ter tek piss, but when's *tha* done owt darin'? Ah want ter just tek a step beyond—beyond borin' normality!'

Moggy could sound very dark at times. The teachers tried to work on him, to get him to take his future more seriously. He might seem, to the uninitiated, like a mass of contradictions: he'd get ninety-nine per cent in a test for German or French, and you knew he'd get nine O levels easily, apparently without opening a book. Yet he'd get into scrapes with the police, running with the local hooligans on a Saturday evening, throwing bottles or bricks at the Wednesday fans.

'Tha'll end up wi' a record. They waen't let thi off again. Tha'll be up before magistrates. Tha'll gerra record and tha waen't gerra job!'

'So ah waen't gerran apprenticeship at British Steel? Worra pity! Thee show me a job rahnd 'ere that's worth 'avin! Trouble wi' thee, Rabbit, tha thinks cos tha'll get thi statutory six fuckin' O levels and keeps thi nose clean tha's cream o' society—but tha not. Tha dun't know 'ow far dahn peckin' order we are, likes o' us!'

I felt chastened by this, though Rabbit, the immediate target of Moggy's scorn, looked indignant merely. Wrapped in his parka, eyes unblinking behind thick horn-rimmed glasses, he seemed impermeable.

Three girls approached, on the other side of the street, one of them known to us. Moggy, diverted from taunting Rabbit, went to the kerb, and called out,

''Ey up, look 'oo's 'ere—local virgins out on town! After a bit o' trouser then, are we?'

'Get stuffed, Moggy—we wouldn't 'ave thee if tha paid us!'

'Why not? Everyone else's 'ad you lot fer nowt!'

Moggy's hoarse dry laugh cracked the cold air. The girls ignored him—Moggy was all talk, you could sense them thinking: all big ideas, none of which would ever bear fruit. They passed by. You could hear their voices fading up the hill, in accents of derision.

We'd reached the edges of the estate by now, close to the industrial districts and the motorway, about a mile from the area of cheap private housing where we all lived (just above the town, in the pock-marked foothills of the Pennines). A little further down, after a steep grassy embankment, you reached the main road into Sheffield, passing through an inferno of dark factories, dingy suburbs of dirty brick terraces and run-down shops, areas of waste ground scattered with weeds, and here and there a chapel, a pub, or an old school building. You could hear the factories very clearly on that crisp night of November 4th, nineteen seventy-four; you would not hear them now.

We had stopped and were silent for a moment, save for the hushed sound of our breathing as we exhaled our dragon-breaths of frosted air. And Moggy had found his car. It stood in a dark dead-end just before the embankment, away from the nearest streetlamp and not directly overlooked by any of the lighted windows of the council flats. It was an Anglia, about six or seven years old. There was an RAC road map on the back window ledge, like the one my father had (on seeing this I began thinking up excuses, to counter the accusations of some imagined interrogator: it wasn't my idea, I was an observer only, never a participant).

'Tha not gonna do it really, are tha, Moggy?'

The tone in Rabbit's voice was one of mild disgust and disapprobation, almost condescension: the voice of some stolid moral majority. I didn't really know which way I wanted things to go. But I didn't quite have Rabbit's instinctive commitment to the conventional, and there was a kind of half-thought, or a suspicion of a thought, somewhere in the back of my mind, that maybe Moggy was reaching for some wild freedom which I also wanted. In which case, I was willing to be led.

'Wanna bet? Thee watch!'

He took the egg out of his pocket. He was wearing an imitation leather jacket which, in a certain light, or absence of light, made him look a convincing hoodlum. I was shivering now. I kept looking around. Rabbit was standing aside, ready to make himself scarce. Moggy wasn't going to rush things: he was almost ceremonious.

Silently, Rabbit and I watched him raise his hand above the bonnet of the Anglia, then pause for a moment. You could hear a kid shouting in the distance, a train rattling along the line towards Sheffield. Then, bringing his arm down in a sweep like an executioner, he dashed the egg on the bonnet. The multiple cracking of the shell seemed magnified in the cold and emptiness of the cul-de-sac.

Rabbit turned away and started to walk. He looked like he wanted a quick getaway. Moggy seemed far away and vacant, emptied. I just stood there watching as bits of shell and pungent yolk and albumen, the lank spillage of Moggy's pointless transgression, slid down the bonnet of the car.

Then Moggy came to and asked me,

'Tha'll 'ave ter confess this, waen't tha,thee bein' Catholic n' that?'

The sheer awkwardness of confessing this escapade to Father Durkan—who came, for added inconvenience, from the same parish in County Mayo as my father—struck me as something to be avoided, by whatever sophistry I might muster.

'No I waen't—it warn't me as did it!'

'So tha says—but thee n' me, we're same, underneath, aren't we?'

I didn't answer, accepting Moggy's question as rhetorical. There was silence again. Rabbit, a few yards away from us by now, turned and looked at us suspiciously.

'Better be goin' then,' he said, from his distance.

'It's only ten past nine!' I said, suddenly animated, having submerged any qualms about my own complicity in Moggy's ritual vandalism. There was no need for anxiety now—no coppers, no irate householder, no strapping young steelworker whose first car had just been wantonly defiled. Moggy had done what he seemed to have to do, no retribution appeared imminent, and now there was this great, unaccountable feeling of release, of being subject to no limits or restraints.

Moggy didn't say anything. But I knew where he was heading, as he walked away from the car. I knew without asking. He didn't take the road back up through the council estate towards home. He took a turning off that road instead; I was walking in step with him as if by instinct, Rabbit following a few paces behind.

There was a little pathway—a *snicket*, to use the local word—which cut through the boundaries of the estate and led up to an ancient area of common land, mostly scrubland with a few stunted trees and bushes and low hillocks and bearing the scars of long-abandoned industrial activities. The neighbourhood's highest point was there. It was a place I had mythologized as a child, staring at it from my bedroom window and inventing a fabulous city there, with high walls and towers, palaces, and secluded courtyards. Later, a moody adolescent, I would go for walks there. Schoolkids would ride mopeds along its dusty paths, go birds-nesting, smoke and drink. You could see it from certain of the school classrooms, a prospect of freedom that seemed ugly and beautiful simultaneously, its ancient industrial spoil heaps alternating with unkempt fields and banks full of weeds. On bright spring and summer days, you would often see skylarks and kestrels there, even sometimes a goldfinch or a linnet (Moggy's grandfather used to keep a linnet in a cage, so Moggy once told me). Sometimes I dream I'm there now, sitting on some vantage point and looking out at the curious half-village, half-suburb where I was born and raised, seeing it still as it was nearly half a century ago; a place you might consider inadequate and yet somehow a portal to infinity, if you knew how to look.

'I want ter look at stars!' Moggy said, at last. He spoke with a sudden show of spirit and enthusiasm, though it sounded almost as though he were choking something back. Rabbit was with us still, perhaps more out of duty than eagerness. I began to quiz Moggy.

'How come tha knows so much about stars, Moggy? Tha even knows their names! Can tha teach me? Come on—name 'em fer us! What's that 'n there, then?'

'There's more than there's names fer. We only see a fraction—in one tiny bit o' one galaxy. Don't even see 'em as they are now—light teks that long ter get 'ere. Tha seein' summat that might even be long gone. Look!'

We'd scrambled up on clumps of coarse grass to the highest of the hillocks. Now Moggy had his arms outstretched, palms upwards and gazing star-wards, as if in supplication. Rabbit's hands were stuffed into his parka. He looked cold.

I looked up too and seemed to see them for the first time ever—a whole diamond scatter of them: such an abundance of stars as seemed almost indecent. And I noticed too how beyond the brighter ones, if you stared hard enough, you saw layer upon layer of other fainter stars, dusted across the sky behind them: an infinite regression of suns and worlds, uncountable and immeasurable.

''ardly matters what their names are—but ah'll tell thi a few, seein' as tha wants ter learn. See Orion, there? No, not there—*there*: follow mi finger. That 'un, top left, that's Betelgeuse. Bottom right, there—

94

that's Rigel. Further ovver there—no, a bit further—Aldebaran. And right dahn there, just above yon tree—that's Sirius. All my stars!'

I couldn't say anything and didn't really want to. Rabbit was looking doubtfully at Moggy, as if he now knew, for certain, that Moggy was mad—which I suppose by many people's standards he was. I wished at that moment that I could be mad too.

The wind was starting up and it was getting colder. Rabbit broke the silence.

'Best be goin' 'ome. Folk'll think we're a bit funny, stood up 'ere at night—if they see us, like'

We scrambled back down the hill and walked towards home, past the secondary school we all attended. There were bits of grit in my shoes, irritating my feet as I walked. As we passed the school grounds, Moggy picked up a large stone and threw it over the high fence into the netball courts. Then we moved on, in silence, to where the streetlights returned, the stars occluded once more by their sulphurous glare.

2022 CYGNATURE SHORT STORY PRIZE

Cygnature Short Story Prize Judge
Katherine Mezzacappa

*M*olly *Bloom at University.* In many ways this isn't an easy story, but then why should a story be 'easy'? Out of a strong field—I had a private shortlist of four—it was the one that resonated most and continued to do so, long after reading. It is Joycean, whilst having a sustained voice all of its own—and bear in mind that I admire Joyce whilst not being a particular fan of his. It's an episode in the life of a probably first-year student, away from home for the first time, living in overpriced accommodation with too many others, who goes to a party. That might sound commonplace enough, but the telling of it isn't. I have not been the age the protagonist is for approximately four decades, but the writer has captured the terror of that age, the physical anxiety about fitting in, the yearning for parents who are not there, who probably were never really there. The heightened, almost hallucinogenic imagery is extraordinary—'the kind of house that has eyes and lips, and an impossible noise, nostrils filled with cement' and 'streetlights…hung like apples pumped full of preservatives.'

Runner up is *Spirit Level,* the dark tale of a small boy of separated parents, whose father is logical, pragmatic but fatally doesn't know the limits of his own expertise. The mother pathologically craves attention which she finds in taking the boy to a series of spiritualist meetings, where she deliberately and consistently shifts the focus of the meeting to herself through a series of lies she herself appears to believe.

The standard of entries was again very high. Quite a few, beyond those I had chosen, would be publishable without changing a comma. These would have been winners on a different day—and are winners. Subject matter was almost universally sombre, perhaps a reflection of our times and the tough challenges faced by the incoming generation. There is grief, loneliness, displacement, death—sometimes by suicide or by murder—nightmares, homophobia. There is love at its most lyrical, and love never expressed. There is the apparently humdrum quotidian, but in the hands of these writers it never is humdrum, alongside speculative fiction. There is a strong showing for dystopia too. What all these stories have in common is originality. I never had the impression of reading something where the author was trying to be something or someone he or she wasn't. I must also salute the courage of all those who entered this competition. Even though the entries were judged blind, and their writers knew that it takes considerable self-belief to put one's own work out in the world. I couldn't have done it, not at their age. I still find it difficult. So, keep going, all of you.

Molly Bloom at University
Eve Naden

Six rooms, four boys. Six rooms with grey walls. Four boys in sweatpants. Four boys and two girls and I'm one of those girls but not the other, because the other is a young woman named Anna who has green hair and works the nightshift at KFC. I can sit in my room and listen to the boys playing GTA in the kitchen, and I can sit in my room and listen to Anna upstairs, walking from her desk to the sink. We all have one desk (laminated wood) and one sink (naked porcelain), and we all have one bed, but my bed sinks towards the middle and I didn't bring any under sheets, but I'm too proud to tell Mum that I haven't packed enough, and I don't want to leave the room (Room 6 out of 6) because there're four boys downstairs and one girl upstairs and I'm afraid they'll hear me. I hear them too, but each sound is unapologetic because they've lived here since the first term and I'm in my final year, but I am bare and stumbling and they walk on solid ground. If I go to the kitchen, I'll expire.

Downstairs, the kitchen is Sunset Boulevard. Everyone is star-studded. Black, white, and grey. Idols. Each housemate has a star on the Hollywood Walk of Fame. And I walk across the landing with nails in my shoes. Everything aches. The blue carpet drowns itself. It's a new carpet and a blue carpet and it's a deep blue, like the ocean, but wilder. The carpet is the colour of mouthwash and I'm sure if I got on my knees and licked it, I'd taste spearmint and elderflower. On the mouthwash carpet, I hear movement from the kitchen, and I have five heart attacks in quick succession before returning to my room with the same mouthwash carpet. My room with a double bed and empty shelves because I'm frightened that my books will send them crashing. I haven't brought enough books anyway and an empty shelf is better than a half-filled one. My books are yellow, creased paperbacks. All cracked spines and folded corners. I'm convinced they were previously owned by chiropractors. I have copies of *The Secret History, Sherlock Holmes,* Kate Atkinson, and there's *Moby Dick* (which I'll never read) and *Moby Dick* will never read me. Above the books and the shelves, there's a corkboard without pins. I didn't bring any pins for this corkboard, and I refuse to ask our landlord, who wears flat caps and riding boots and owns seventeen houses while I will never own one. There's a text from my landlord who wears flat caps, on my desk below the empty shelves. I think about reading it as I change into a ratty jumper spotted with zodiac symbols. The jumper stretches; it pockets my skin like a secret, and I wish I could keep myself secret for the rest of my degree, but I blurt, and shout and I've already told one of my housemates about the mole on my back and why my father doesn't love me. My father doesn't love me, and I stare at my body because that's one of the reasons. And my body is stuffed into pyjamas which don't fit and I'm still wearing a bra, though it's decorative; there's so little support it might as well be a glorified sock. I think about telling Mum all this, but my phone is charging, and I haven't checked how thin the walls are and if my housemates will hear me cry. And I shouldn't text Mum otherwise she'll get messages every two weeks asking whether a *Rolling Stones* T-Shirt belongs in a darks wash or a coloureds wash and then another text five minutes later saying, don't worry I've figured it out when of course I haven't, and the clothes will remain unwashed. Unwashed clothes means Amazon. I sit with Amazon on my chest, propped against a stained pillow. The pillow is stained with coffee, splotches shaped like the real Amazon. The pillow is flat—I can feel the headboard beneath it—but I curl my neck to scroll. I order skinny fit jeans. I order scented candles I can't light in case I set fire to the house and lose my £600 pound deposit. I order crayons, tattoo sleeves, silver-plated earrings. I send them to the wrong address. Then I change the address and order perfume bottles, wax figurines, handmade bookmarks, neon dreamcatchers, men's underwear. I eat crisps on my lap whilst buying things I'll never use. I watch romantic films on mute because I want to check if I'm broken and strange and malformed, or frigid as Sam called me when I told him no. I tell Sam he's wrong as I stare at the ceiling and try to masturbate, with little success. I unlock the door, hoping one of my housemates will walk in and say, oh look, there's a cool girl, there's a girl who knows what she's doing, there's a girl like the ones I masturbate to. And even if Project Masturbation is a success, the aftermath will bulge with shame and guilt because I'm alone, because I'm doing this for myself, and there is no one else and it's just me using my own body. My body makes me wish I were a man. My body makes me wish I were a man in tweed who smokes Italian cigars and drinks top-shelf bourbon, though I like neither of those things. I do like tweed. I like the idea of tweed. I see tweed and I picture the gun dog and game fairs Aunty Clare used to drag me to, where women toting riding crops would shoot clay pigeons and talk about horse racing. There's a racetrack near the university, but not near the house and yet I can hear soil churning. I can hear *The Pixies* downstairs. My housemates sing along. My housemates sing till they send Aaron to find me, and Aaron doesn't knock. He doesn't knock, but he wears leather jackets. He wears those jackets and say things like 'lit' and 'tight' which I'm sure taste different in his mouth. There are two beer cans in the pockets of his denim shirt. He looks so unassuming that I hate him.

'You coming to the party?' he asks.

'Yeah. I go to parties all the time,' I say. He laughs and rubs his stubbly chin.

'It's nothing much,' he says. 'Just a few of Luke's friends. You might know them. They're studying English as well.'

I stand on the threshold; my door is open. My door is gaping. He can see inside. It's the same reason I never open the fridge if someone's looking, or my cupboard in the kitchen or the front door. Aaron shrugs.

'You don't have to come,' he says, but of course I am coming. I ask him what I should bring, and he says it's a house party, not a holiday. A house party just down the road, and we're on the stairs now; the stairs are one large corkscrew. Luke is at the bottom of the stairs, a fag tucked behind his ear. His ears are large, and kite-shaped. Luke says I should bring beer.

'Or vodka,' he adds. 'Vodka is good too. We'll stop at the shops on the way there. It's only a five-minute walk.'

The five-minute walk takes place in the dark; the alien glare of the corner shop is oddly comforting. I am swept up in queues of people the university advertised as being like-minded. These like-minded people become fish in a tunnel. I am swept down this tunnel with my back pressed against the fridge. Against the fridge, which emits a Tim Burton glow, I am limited to grabbing whatever I see. I find two cans of gin and tonic and a rum and coke. The gin, the rum. I swipe a bag of sweets. I don't know what kind of sweets are in my hand because I'm pushed to the till and asked to produce my ID and the cashier doesn't seem to realise that it's a loaded question, asking someone for their ID. The man checking my ID has a muskrat moustache which wriggles; I'm sure he knows I'm the girl who once thought Wetherspoons was posh. I wouldn't sell alcohol to me either. The alcohol sloshes as I pass it over, and he scans each barcode, asks for ID again because I didn't give it to him the first time. The first sip, I take with the boys outside. The alcohol which sloshed around in its cans now sloshes around in my belly. I hold the cans like I'm holding mugs of hot chocolate—both hands clasped around the cylinders. I'm convinced Luke and Aaron will judge the brands I bought, the type of alcohol I'm drinking, when the reality is that they probably don't care, just like Anna probably doesn't care whether I cook bacon noodles or microwave a Shepherd's Pie. The road is burnt like that Shepherd's Pie as we walk to the house. The boys walk in tandem. I lag as they walk in tandem. They're walking together and I'm perpetually catching up. Catching up when they reach the house, which is a simple redbrick semi-detached near the Old Vic Pub. Near the pub, it's the kind of house that has eyes and lips, and an impossible nose, nostrils filled with cement. Those nostrils expand as the door opens, producing a lanky Asian kid who introduces himself as Leo. Leo the lion with his freshly dyed hair; he carries a beer like it needs swaddling. Leo the lion roars to let us in. Aaron, Luke, and me—all are welcome.

'Come on in,' says Leo. I want to hide inside his mane. His mane ruffles as he raises his head, greeting Luke and Aaron with a 'hey, man, what's up, not bad, how you been, you got the stuff?'

There's Leo, Luke, Aaron, and a crowd of us, packed into this cardboard living room. The living room isn't a living room. The living room is stasis and presence, where 18–25-year-olds mill about in a smoky haze, listening to *Queen*. Most are drunk. Most lie back with cat-like smiles—happy drunk. They are happy drunks, and I am barely drunk but sad drunk and tipsy drunk and wondering why I came. Wondering why I came whilst trying to remember the bands Aaron likes and the books Luke is studying. Luke is also studying a girl's body; she leans against the wall sipping rum. She's sipping rum with lips of clay, her neck caked with make-up.

'Sit down,' she says. 'You can fit four on that sofa.'

Four people are already on that sofa, but I don't say this. Instead, I squeeze myself in the middle of the four, right between Aaron and some blonde man with an inexplicably ginger beard. Ginger beard and legs spread, wearing a white shirt and a crucifix. The metal jangles as he sits up, turns to me, asks me if I'm here with anyone even though he's just seen me come in. We've just come in, but Luke is dancing. Luke is dancing with this girl he's been studying, hands in his pockets. Not dancing then. I'm not sure how you can dance with your hands in your pockets, not without falling over. If he falls, I'm sure he'll bounce straight back up. Continue dancing. I want to ask someone to dance, but I wonder if someone's cock will shrivel because I'm a girl and I'm asking them when they feel they should be asking me. But no one will ask me and besides, Luke's not dancing anymore. Instead of dancing, he's tipping cocaine onto the coffee table. The coffee table is glass. The glass coffee table is now repurposed; it's modern art. Gather round. As Luke draws lines with the white powder, I want to ask where he got it, wondering who'd make deals with a twenty-something Literature student who reads Proust for fun and wears an alarming range of *Led Zeppelin* T-Shirts. For some reason, I think drug dealers do lots of research on their clients. And Luke is one of their clients and he's snorting the stuff while I chat with Aaron about whether T.S. Eliot's *Tradition and the Individual Talent* is pedestrian.

I leave the party early. I leave the party; it's early enough that cars are circling the roads. I follow the streetlights, which hang like apples pumped full of preservatives. I follow the apple-lights and I think about calling Mum, who will be in bed anyway, so there's no point calling her at all. I follow the lights and don't call anyone. There's no one to call when I reach the house—everyone is asleep or out at a different party, so I prepare for tomorrow's workshop, reading endless journal articles which mansplain how a passage from Hope Mirrlees's *Paris* represents her fear of vaginas, but I stop reading half-way through because a poem is a poem is a poem.

A poem is a poem, and I am a poem. One of those half-formed modernist poems, all fragments. Bits of bad grammar, caps lock, and typography which make no sense. I'm supposed to be all new-age and sexy, but I'm a strange half-formed thing. A half-formed thing lying in bed listening to Playlists to Cry to at 2 am though it's neither 2 am nor am I crying. I am not crying but listening or trying not to listen as Anna fucks Luke in the upstairs bathroom. She cries out a few times and I wonder what it's like—to make such noise with abandon. When they abandon their abandon and return to their rooms, I stick my head out the door. Listen to the silence. Breathe in before it's trampled by Aaron on the stairs. I duck back into the room, clutching my bladder. My bladder isn't the issue here: I haven't shit in days. Not in the house, never in the house have I taken a shit. If I feel the need, I'll walk twenty minutes to campus and pick a disabled loo where I can sit heaving for as long as I like without fear of interruption. Fearful of interruptions, my arsehole has become shy. And my bones strain, skin bulging as I realise I'm holding myself hostage. In this house with the rent and the four boys and one girl and me, taking myself prisoner for £628 a month.

I lock the door and decide I'll shit tomorrow because tomorrow I need to wash my hair and one of the bathrooms has a shower and a toilet, so I'll run the shower while I shit and mute the sound of being human. The sound of cracking as I climb into bed, brushing crumbs onto the carpet. The carpet is too bright. Too bright and I want to switch the lights off but I'm already in bed. In bed, I'm telling myself that I'm still writing, and I've done all my reading for the following week. I haven't missed one seminar; I went to a party where a twenty-three-year-old man pissed out the window. I didn't dance, but I drank. Drinking with the housemates, who are downstairs watching *The Social Network* and laughing because Michael Cera is perfect casting. It's all perfect because they're downstairs and I can go to the loo, and I can be alone and bask in the thought that I am alone, and they are downstairs.

And then I watch a film about young love, where two perfect specimens hold each other and become a single shape. I start to cry, so that's something.

2022 BEDFORD SHORT STORY
PRIZE WINNER

Bedford Short Story Prize Judge's Report
Guy Russell

This was my second time judging The Bedford Short Story Prize, and once again it was a fun and eye-opening experience to discover what varied and sometimes startling stuff the writers of Bedfordshire are producing.

My eagerly awaited batch this year had no lack of sinister twists, domineering parents, dream sequences, bereavement, relationship troubles and family secrets. And the supernatural was an especially frequent element. In the very first story I picked up, a couple at a restaurant where a conjuror is working the tables slowly realize his tricks really *are* magic. In another, a woman in a coffee-shop meets a paranormal stranger who tells her, 'You are not dead. But you are not living.' And another clever tale used the tradition of the corn-dolly, whose 'spirit of the wheat' alleviates a son's loneliness after his mother's death.

Of the science-fiction entries, my favourite was set in a post-apocalyptic society where the narrator works in the Re-Edification Bureau, rewriting classic literature so that it conforms to 'The Truth'. He's just done *Pilgrim's Progress* and is asked to start on *Animal Farm*... Its satirical humour was lovely, and its world-building was so detailed it felt like the start of a novel.

In one of the most horrifying pieces, the protagonist wakes to find himself in a professional torture room complete with mid-floor drainage channel, where his gradual awareness of his helplessness and his torturer's business-like vindications ('my job is to carry out the client's wishes') made for chilling reading.

On a less grim note, there was plenty of romance. An eccentric man-in-a-tree falls in love with a dog-walker. A young lad who's been instructed that he should 'always keep to the path' leaves it one day and meets an attractive shop assistant. A housewife *almost* has a fling with her plasterer. And I really enjoyed the story in which *Brief Encounter* is viewed from the perspective of Ethel, waitress at the station tea-room, who is also occupied with her own more conventional courtship.

Anyway, it's probably clear by now that it wasn't easy to find a winner. If I could have awarded a second place, it would have gone to *Sleeping on the Wing*, a stylish tale with a nicely paced finish in which Ava (Latin=*avis*, bird), a commuter still grieving from her husband's death, watches a sleeping man in her carriage, sees the swifts flying outside, and begins to dream she's one of them.

However, I'd like to give the prize to the terrific *Troubled Nights* for the deft way it manages to mix domestic comedy, horror, oneiricism and romance, and for its lively characterisations and vivid similes ('the lifeless limb swung to and fro like a slowing pendulum'). I also really enjoyed its construction: from a gentle start, it delivers an increasing pace, several clever surprises and a happy (and witty) ending.

So special congratulations to this particularly talented writer. I've felt honoured to judge the prize and would like to thank the organisers for asking me, and for all the work that makes it possible. Finally, I'd like to thank all the entrants, and to say to those Bedfordians who didn't win, or didn't get round to entering, or never even thought of entering but *do* have a(nother) good story deep in a folder of the PC: get it out and revise it; there's next year coming up.

Troubled Nights
Jesse Perrin

With no time to react, the front door slammed to a close behind her. 'Damn,' said Polly Brown, finding herself locked out in the middle of a chilly autumn night, all because old Megan Smith from next door was banging on the wall again.

Standing in the recessed front porch of the Victorian terraced dwelling, Polly shivered as much in surprise at her sudden predicament as in the cold. A full moon provided the only illumination, casting everything black or grey, the dull contrasts replacing the daylight reds and blues of tiles laid in herringbone pattern in the porch and along the short garden path which led into the street. Feint shadows of ornate lampposts imposed their exaggerated shapes on the street pavement and on the now greyed redbrick facades of the dwellings opposite.

Bleary-eyed, no make-up, hair in a mess and skimpily dressed in only a short cotton nightie and flip-flops, the young woman was at least thankful for the partial darkness. She wouldn't want gorgeous new neighbour Lionel from across the way to see her in such a state. She had got off to a good start when by chance they had met at the corner shop, he reaching to a top shelf and handing her down a bacon brunch. It was important to be looking her best. Lionel was tall, slim, and always immaculately dressed in the latest fashion. He smelt nice too. With wavy short black hair, an alluring face and gentlemanly demeanour, he was the new subject of Polly's vivid dreams; quite a change from the lustful rake of her last liaison, a middle-aged Peter Pan who wore garish open chested shirts, ripped jeans, jewellery, and had more hands than a ship's crew.

Stepping over the stub blue-brick wall which separated the two dwellings, Polly found herself on Megan's front doorstep. Batty old woman, she thought, waking me up in the middle of the night.

She ought to be in a home.

Megan Smith never slept well at night. Too many daytime naps, Polly reckoned. The old woman blamed it on the house. It had been different when Herbert was alive, even though he had been more married to his job at the bank than he ever was to her. She had found him dead on the landing, kneeling forward, slumped against the closed bathroom door, with both hands still gripping the handle.

Polly rapped the large eagle-headed brass knocker on Megan's door, the impact opening it as though an invisible hand had invited entry.

'Megan. Are you there?' Polly said, straining her head round the gaping door.

'Is that you, Polly? Do come in,' came the distant reply.

Polly stepped inside and pushed the door to a close behind her. She flicked a shiny brass switch on the wall, and somewhere down the narrow, musty hallway, a dismal orange lamp hanging from a twisted flex started to glow, barely relieving the darkness.

The constant banging which had broken Polly's sleep had left her disorientated, with a residue of wishful dreams still lingering. Alone in the chilly, dark hallway, the anger which had emboldened her to venture out and tear a strip off the old woman had gone. Now she felt frightened. Perhaps Megan is right, she thought. This place is spooky. Maybe it is the house.

'In here, Polly,' Megan's voice called out from the front parlour. Polly took a few hesitant steps down the hall. Grasping the small brass-ball handle of the partially open parlour door, she entered the room. In the semi-darkness sat what appeared to be a large, pitch-black lion, proudly sitting at rest. Catching her breath before fully recognising the familiar object, Polly stepped round it. It was the large chaise-longue, its front facing the fireplace on the other side of the room. Supine on its long leather seat lay the tiny form of Megan Smith, wrapped tightly in a fleecy blanket and resting her night-capped head on a folded white bolster. On the tiled hearth, a small gas fire stood issuing the barest of heat and sole source of illumination from its cracked ceramic radiant.

Polly knew the old lady preferred the dark, not wishing to be reminded of the years she had sat in silence staring at the heavily embossed patterned paper decaying on the walls, while Herbert, sitting opposite, would have his head constantly buried in a large workbook, fascinated by its content.

'Oh, Polly, thank goodness you have come. I'm half out my wits,' the old lady said. 'What is it this time, Megan?' Polly asked. 'Why do you keep banging on the wall?' 'No, Polly, that wasn't me,' Megan replied. 'It was the doors, lots of slamming doors. '

'Which doors? Where?' Polly said.

'Through there,' Megan replied, pointing at the living room door.

'But there's only the French doors through there,' Polly said. 'And they step out on to the garden patio.'

'No, no, Polly, there are more rooms than that. Empty rooms, rooms without windows, doors with big brass handles. I can never find my way out.'

The woman's a proper basket case, Polly thought.

'Now listen to me, Megan,' Polly said. 'I will sit right here in this chair until it gets light.

'Alright?'

'You are so good to me coming round like this, Polly dear,' Megan replied.

Polly wanted to say, *I've got no choice if I want to get a bit of peace and quiet.* But she said nothing, feeling sorry for the old woman.

Megan turned her back to the fire and, with a deep sigh, settled down to sleep.

Polly picked up the old lady's redundant nightgown from the end of the chaise-longue and wrapped it around her own shoulders. She slumped into the leather armchair close by Megan's makeshift bed, too distant from the paltry fire to gain any sensation of warmth.

On the floor by the chair where Polly sat, a large, black, hardback book entitled Bank Vaulting

Systems lay open. A compulsive reader, the young woman picked it up and began to flip the pages. In the darkness it was difficult to see the words, but she could make out the exploded pictures on each page, revealing the inner workings of the strongest bank vaults. Good grief, she thought. Some of those doors are a foot thick. And those enormous handles must take some turning. She wondered why Megan could find nothing better to read than one of Herbert's old workbooks. No wonder she was going off her trolley.

In the dim light, Polly managed to turn just a few pages before her tired eyes started to close.

She drifted towards sleep, thinking of her next chance meeting with Lionel.

In that mental mangle of transition between reality and dreams, Polly felt something unexpected. It was Megan's hand gripping her arm. The old lady was standing by the side of the chair, at first silent as a ghost, then quietly urging, 'Come, Polly dear. We must get away from this place.'

'Please go back to sleep, Megan,' Polly said with instant irritability at being torn from slipping into a lovely dream.

'No, we must not sleep,' the old lady urged.

'But why not?' Polly asked.

'The doors. The slamming doors,' Megan said. 'And that hideous presence. We must go now.'

'Go where?' Polly asked. 'And what hideous presence?'

'I don't know, but we must get away.'

'Please get back on the chaise-longue and go to sleep,' Polly said in a manner not inviting refusal.

'But there is no time,' Megan said. 'We must go before it is too late.' She gripped her guardian's arm even tighter and began to pull, her action so desperate that Polly became alarmed. Without further protest she rose from her chair. She knew the shortest way out of the house and, with the old woman still clinging fast, made towards the living room door.

'No! Not that way, Polly. Not that way.' Megan called out, letting go of her would-be helper.

'Don't distress yourself, Megan. You must follow me closely,' Polly said. She felt the trembling touch of the old lady's cold hand on her back, seeking closeness and reassurance. Polly faltered for a moment when she thought of the words she had uttered in her last command. She now realised that when attempting to leave Megan's house by the living room, it would be the first time she had ventured beyond the slabbed limestone patio, that spread out like an apron in front of the French doors. There remained unexplored the long-forgotten garden of

114

shrubs and small trees that Herbert used to so carefully tend, which had now run wild. Was there a gated opening somewhere in the wall? Polly wondered. She wouldn't ask Megan, for the old woman, not wishing to take another step in the direction they were going, was bound to say no.

It was the first time Polly had noticed the big brass doorknob on the living room door. Surely it wasn't there on her previous visit. She found it difficult to turn but managed to open the door. As she stepped into semi-darkness, the door slammed to a close behind her. She could no longer feel Megan's hand and knew without looking back that the old lady had not made it into the room, only her muted cries seeping through the dense oak of the door. As Polly turned, trying in vain to open the slammed door, Megan's cries finally subsided.

I must get out of this damned house, Polly thought. *Megan will just have to look after herself.*

'This is not the living room,' Polly muttered to herself as she peered into the gloom of a long, narrow, windowless space. She groped the wall for a light switch which did not exist. At the far end of the room, in a vague glimmer of light with no apparent source, she could just see the outline of a door. She decided to make haste towards it.

'I knew it. This must be it,' she said with instant relief, coming up to the door and expecting at any moment to step out on to the patio. First there was another big brass knob to turn. Reluctant to touch it but convinced it would be her means of escape, Polly grasped it with both hands, hoping to turn it rapidly. It was even more difficult to turn than the last one. In the intolerable delay, panic set in. She became aware of a presence behind her but was too frightened to look back.

With waning strength, the young woman finally turned the knob and stepped into another dim room. Again, the door behind her slammed shut, and there far ahead stood the figure of a man in silhouette, standing by yet another door. He was beckoning Polly to come over. She recognised immediately the outline of Lionel; that tall, upright stature and welcoming wave. Desperate and besotted, she ran towards her would-be rescuer and lover. As she got nearer, the soupy blackness of the room began to clear, revealing Lionel's features. He was leering, with evil intent in his eyes.

Uncertain and repelled by what she saw, Polly halted. The rest of

Lionel then lit up like a rabbit caught in headlights, exposing every feature. His greasy, matted, long grey hair, and ripped black jeans held up with a spike-studded white belt which cradled a tattooed medicine-ball paunch proudly bursting through his sweat-drenched open grey shirt. And around his neck a gold medallion swung pendulously across the grey hairs of his fake tan chest. He said not a word. Between the thumb and forefinger of his raised right hand he held a familiar front door key, silently beckoning Polly to take it. She tried to speak, but could only mouth, 'So that's your game. And I thought you were different.'

On much weakened legs she turned to flee, trying desperately to return from this journey into hell. The presence which had followed her was still there, somehow always behind her, the unseen impetus of her flight. It would be beyond fright to turn and look. She struggled as though wading through treacle, taking an eternity to return to the door through which she had just entered. This time the handle turned, but the door would not open. She became consumed in screaming, her brain exploding into mental fragments that searched out horror in every crevice of the nightmare world around her. She began to wander, half seeing, listening to her own terrible scream until it finally began turning into the sobs of aftermath. Now she was unaware of closed doors or dark rooms. Just a slow, painless retracing of steps back to the parlour. Back to the oblivion of sleep.

In her half-naked state, Polly began to feel cold. The icy leather of the armchair was stinging her bare legs at the slightest movement. Aroused by the sensation, she opened her eyes. She noticed Megan's nightgown lying at the foot of the living room door but was not inclined to return it to her own shoulders, as though denying that any struggle had occurred to explain its changed position.

Face down and askew, the big book lay on the floor by the side of her chair.

Eventually alert enough to bother, Polly looked up to see whether Megan was awake. A shaft of daylight coming through a slit in the closed curtains illuminated the pallid grey of the old woman's face. She was staring fixedly at Polly.

'Good morning, Megan,' Polly said quietly.

The old woman continued to stare.

'Megan. Are you alright? Megan!' Polly sprang from her chair in horror. She grabbed the old woman's cold, stiff arm and began to shake it, frantic at the lack of response.

'Megan! Wake up! Please wake up!' Polly demanded, guessing that to do so, the old lady must first return from the rigour of recent death.

'Oh God, it wasn't a dream. Or am I dreaming still?' Polly said out loud.

In despair, not knowing which world she was in, Polly released her grip on the old woman's arm and stood fixedly, her eyes hypnotically attracted to the lifeless limb as it swung to and fro like a slowing pendulum, brushing against the smooth, frictionless leather of the chaise-longue until coming to rest with a momentary life-mimicking jerk.

Polly waited, resigned to be transported by reality or dream to an unknown fate. She did not have long to wait. With the predictability of a nightmare in which one event is followed by another of even greater terror, she heard footsteps in the hall. And they were getting closer. A voice called out:

'Anyone there? I'm coming in?'

'Oh, God, it is a dream after all,' Polly muttered. She would recognise that hideous Lionel's voice anywhere. 'That dodgy latch has let in the devil.'

With nowhere to hide, she ran screaming at the half open parlour door, hoping to shut out her tormentor. Before she could reach it, the door opened wide and, Lionel, perfectly dressed in a dark blue silk dressing gown and tan leather slippers, appeared in the opening. His only concession to a state of dishevelment was the growth of a few hours of stubble on his handsome face.

Unseeing, Polly slammed into her tormentor. As she did so, Lionel flung his arms around her to keep his balance. Pressed together, they stood fast, hearts thumping, waiting for the shock of collision to subside and winded lungs to re-fill.

'Polly! What on earth's the matter?' Lionel gasped.

'Please tell me I'm dreaming,' Polly pleaded.

'No Polly, you are not dreaming, but holding you like this I think I could be.'

117

The familiar scent of Old Spice filled Polly's nostrils. She began to feel safe in Lionel's embrace.

Lionel said, 'The old lady's front door was ajar, so I thought I'd better come and see if everything was all right.'

Polly sobbed, 'If only my front door had a dodgy latch. I could have got back in.'

She tried to explain about the constant banging on the wall and how she had rushed out in the middle of the night to give old Megan a piece of her mind. 'I thought I might as well stay the night after locking myself out,' Polly said, adding, 'Oh, Lionel. If only you knew what I have been through.'

'Polly darling, there's nothing to worry about now,' Lionel replied. 'I'll ring for a locksmith later. He can kill two birds with one stone.'

With Polly not wanting Lionel to release his passionate hold, it was some moments before she cried out, 'Please don't say there is nothing to worry about. Look. Megan is dead.'

In the semi-darkness and facing the high back of the chaise-longue, Lionel had been unaware of the resting body, which was still mostly hidden under the blanket.

At Polly's mention of the old lady's name, the blanket moved.

'Did someone say I'm dead? Megan asked, raising her cold, dangling arm and tucking it under the blanket. 'I do hope not,' she added. 'I did have an awful time dropping off to sleep, but then I slept like a log. Herbert used to say he could wake the dead easier than he could wake me. I trust you had a good night, Polly my dear?'

Out of sight, and with her hands round Lionel's waist and her eyes looking longingly into his, Polly replied, 'Oh yes, Megan. It turned out to be quite beyond my wildest dreams.'

2022 POETRY COMPETITION

Poetry Competition Judge's Report
Jessica Mookherjee

How do you judge a poetry competition? I was very honoured to be asked to undertake this task for The Bedford Poetry Competition and knowing that the ethos of the competition is to spread the joy of writing and poetry as well as support a host of good causes is also important to me. Thank you to all who entered. You keep the poetry world alive.

I was asked to do a number of things—create a long list of the 40 best poems, and then a short list of 12 and from this discover the eventual winners. Reading the poems over a number of weeks was like meeting new people. I wondered how is it possible to compare one glorious person to another—each with their own rich flavours, contexts and possibilities? I had to concede this is no perfect science. So I found some refuge in what I believe poetry is. I had to remind myself that a poem itself is a bubble of reality, a crafted creation and there is something a poem does that no other work of art does.

Longlist

Is that a way to judge I thought? To ask, has the poem created a single world for me? There were so many beautiful poems about heartbreaking situations—often watching our loved ones fade and die, broken hearts and holidays past remembered. However, some poems created uneasy worlds with vivid images, holding metaphors and themes about lives almost lived, the world's tragedies and victories—all these worlds are ripe for poetry, but it is the poet's job to use the theme and form and imagery in a careful balance. Has the poem been crafted so it can stand up? And by that I mean does its form work for it or against it? There were some poems that I loved but appeared in a form that made me question them—perhaps like a person whose laughter appears too forced but is still funny. There were some poems whom I just wanted to love but perhaps we were a little incompatible and these were the poems that I felt were not quite finished. There were many in the long list that had excellent lines, impressive themes and images and yet somehow missed an edit, where the ending had been missed, where the poet had missed their own beauty. There were many poems I met that I would love to read in that poet's collection, surrounded but other supporting poems but yet…somehow on their own—amidst an array of other people's poems—felt a little lonely or not quite shining in their own light. For these poems I send love, because I often think my own poems are like that—they often need to be surrounded by their brother and sister poems for them to live fully. Many of the poems in the long list were those poems, that I know will appear in collections and with a little tweak here and there will find their way to magazines and perhaps even win again.

Shortlist

The 12 poems that ended up in my shortlist were the poems that stayed with me. They were often poems I had interesting relationships with over a course of weeks. One of the poems in the short list I was clear at first that I wasn't going to short list at all, the poem was funny and poignant and I decided at first it was too obviously a poem who I'd go down the pub and might lead me astray with but I kept reading it and decided I just liked its style and wanted it in my life, so that poem—like some people just decided to stick around. So well done to *Seducing Tom Jones at the Travelodge in Slough.* I commend you. There were poems in the shortlist that I loved for their bravery, for some reason they spoke of ancestry and maybe they drew me into a conversation that was bigger than the poem itself, and they used a form that worked for the poem itself. The poem, *The Ancestors Get Questions About Your DNA Test Results,* was one of those—it picks up pace in a relentless incantation. There were two very different poems about identity in the shortlist, quiet, reflective poems, one, *When your Jamaican Grandmother Sings to you,* felt like a lullaby—albeit an uneasy one. I chose two poems for the shortlist that were 'concrete' poems—and these are not my usual taste of poetry at all, however I admired the poets' use of the concrete form—one who created a world that was both uneasy and crafted, *from the dark side,* and another which splayed out a romantic almost mythical city scape in a hard concrete block subverting the harsh reality of city life. There were poems about what we didn't do, or what we discarded, and these poems lingered with me in my thoughts for weeks. My final three took me some time and deliberation and reading and re-reading. Finally, it always comes down to taste— once you have admired the craft and the use of metaphor, image and music inside the work, you are left with the question of which are the poems that you can live with every day and might even become part of you? This is bound to differ depending on the Judge. So, forgive me all shortlisted poems—for you were all my friends.

The final selection: Winners

The poem, *My Mother's Watch,* was not a poem I expected to like, as already I had read so many poems about bereavement, the loss of a parent (all important poems to witness) and I wondered what would this poem have to offer me and when I finished the poem I just cried and wasn't sure why, and I realised the poet has used the short clipped language of time and its own brutality in a blistering unsentimental way, that holds grief in and also crystallises it in the image of the delicate, fragile and precious watch that continues to move and I felt it, I felt a dying mother just gently brush the poets face with a hand. I chose *On A Cold Day In New Orleans* because of the vastness of the poem, the great ambitious sweep of images, like a vast landscape of particulars where the poet seems lost and dislocated and the use of language and form worked with the poet's intention, keeping pace, steady and sweeping as a river, but it was the solitary Ibis that finally drew my attention—the bird standing alone amidst the sweep of the world, like the poet both alone and connected to everything. I look forward to hearing more from this poet. My winner, *The Bees,* completely surprised me and originally did not make the shortlist because there was something in the end line that I needed to take time with, luckily it had lodged inside my brain, and I went back to it for multiple readings and the more I read the more I could hear that buzzing. The way the poet has crafted the work is full of music, the use of the central image mutates and becomes the relationship between two people and a house and transmutes again into the image of the poem itself. A poem about language, sound and what we carry inside us, our relationship to the natural world and our habitat and each other had me compelled. That is what poetry can do that no other art form can do, create a spell inside your body and expel it into the world fully formed, containing things that cannot be spoken in any other way. Well done. Well done to all who entered, for all the beautiful words and it was an honour to witness your creations.

The Bees
Damen O'Brien

The house was talking, and you couldn't sleep.
I heard the sound of fists of rice running
through rough hands, seedpods rattling in a
breeze, if I heard anything at all. You said
you heard the claws of scrabbling rats, the
whispers of angry men. Sneaking things. But
I did not hear that. Perhaps a susurration,
perhaps the wash of foam on bevelled stones.
We prized a chunk of gyprock from the wall,
opened the throat of the house a little more,
and there like the gears of some marvellous
machine, the architectural origami of a hive
of bees, shuttling, whirring, moving through
their purpose, the shape of homely din. So
of course, they had to go, you had to sleep,
you had to stop those night terrors that
would shake you out of restless sleep with the
dragging sound of death. But now you say
you want to put them back, scoop the beady
jitter of their bodies, their fiddly wings back
into the hole, gather up the pour, the spill
of them and close up the breach. You tell me
that you cannot sleep without the sound, but
once we moved the hive the bees won't return,
I told you that they follow on their Queen and
that has comforted you. You do not yawn, but
whenever you open your mouth a bee flies out.

SECOND PLACE

On A Cold Day In New Orleans
G H Plaag

on a cold day in New Orleans, i can see clearly
beyond the swamps, the archipelagos, the plumage
from the grey refineries, their flames, the dust
in the air, the quicklime in the Seventh Ward
foundations, the crumbling infrastructure, the dust
of that slow slip into the mud, the Mississippi
curled like a bicep around the shotguns and the cranes.

from the top of the Huey P. Long Memorial Bridge
(a funny idea) i can see clearly, am seeing
a bed for time to sleep in,
a reaching, an anxious weary eventual
graveyard for the parade day hats
and the souls who wore them like armor,
chainmail glitter, against flattening (but never
beads—those are for the tourists);

i can see clearly with the breath of winter,
the death of lurid things, the draining of color,
the humid freeze
they have been warning me about.
i can see the crystals of the sun warm off
the muddy water,
restless in the shifting switchbacks
of current. i can see that it frosts here, too;
that the summer will end.

i can see clearly the sharp notes of jazz
louvered flat by the flat grey cold
and the old, furrowed doors in the Quarter

closed for repairs; and i can see pelicans,
sometimes, flying home from whatever place,
and American things with French names. i can see
just one ibis on Napoleon Avenue.
just one, alone.

and all these things standing still and wary,
waiting, ears up, like a cat in glass, i can see clearly
with my own eyes, with their own slow haunting,
on this one cold morning.

THIRD PLACE

My Mother's Watch
Norman Goodwin

Each time I pick it up, her thin, gold watch,
I wonder if that second-hand still sweeps
around the tiny face past painted numbers
she no longer sees but wears as if she could.

For a second she sweeps away the hands
that try to lift her body from the bed
and soiled gown she doesn't want to see,
but wears to keep her hip incision clean.

She tries to lift her body from the bed while
tethered to a tube fed up her nose and down
her throat. It keeps her stomach clean since
nothing will stay put but her bad luck.

Tethered to a tube, fed up with hunger,
with an *Ileus,* meaning any drink or solid
won't stay put. It comes back up. Bad luck
unless it leaves, her gut restarts. But say

the *ileus* lingers, solid, no drinks—then what?
Eight days, the clock hands scythe away our hope.
The doctors leave and won't restart her care.
While I sit, bedside in a chair, her breathing stops.

Day eight: a life now scythed away, a hush,
no blinks or beeps, just denial's disbelief.
I pick it up, her thin, gold-plated watch, how
strange to see her second hand still sweeps.

The Ancestors Get Questions About Your DNA Test Results

G R Kramer

Irish, Mongol, some Ashkenazi Jew,
Hopi, Spaniard, a modest dash Bantu.
You thought yourself Bohemian?
Since we live so large in your skull
we see you think you were lied to.
Come to our cave in your headlamp

with questions cast by its weak light.
Wrapped in your thick quilt of fictions
stitched by the thin luminous threads
of molecules and mysteries
that make such dull life. Your suspicion
is mountainous. What coin are you owed—

you who imagine the dismal days
of the dead are spent mining
radioactive half-lies? Child,
we don't care if our story reads straight,
we have nothing to spend but time,
but not time enough to please you.

Your inheritance is a shamble
of science, star waste and love
fused inside chemical spirals,
amoebas mutated to bastards,
blood transfigured from venom,
slave traders costumed as saints.

The geology of life compacts
into strata of lost worlds, squeezes
petty hearts to dust, degenerates

to weary atoms, then repairs
to gold. Like conscious continents,
we break what is broken in us

as we grind chromosomes together,
as the volcanic joins to the glacial,
as the living are tied to the dead,
as a human finds a human in crowds,
something strange glows in the dirt,
the radiant lonely decay of love.

The Daughter You Almost Had
Ricky Ray

Talk to the daughter you almost had,
ask her if her father in neverland is kind,
patient, indulgent of her curiosities,
prone to spoil her behind her mother's back,
and if she goes quiet when you ask,
sit with her until it passes.
That she exists in an old
dream you keep
behind an abandoned desire
is enough true bond to love by.
Tell her you're sorry
you weren't ready to have children, sorrier
you thought there was a point at which
you could be ready. That no one
could replace her. That you're still
ashamed, and trying to love the little ones—
broken vine, caught mouse, wing-bent bird—
who come to you, sorrowing at the precipice
of help or death. And tell her that this time,
not always, but more and more often,
when a soul comes limping,
you think of her,
and you choose the light-switch labeled help.

emptying your wardrobes
Lucy Crispin

A kind of archaeology—strata of being,
revealed. Jammed in amongst the *lunch with the girls* chic,
the carer cardies, here are the holiday clothes,
the shoestring-strap dresses hand-sewn
in the gloom of a 3-day-week Aberdeen winter;
the wind braying in the gas flue, the elements
glowing in the candlelit room.

And here's that soft, soft long green dress—
frilled yoke, full sleeves gathered to the wrist:
the Entertaining Era. Hair and makeup done,
the glitter of earrings, and two small girls who'd snuck
to the bend in the stairs, hearing cutlery on the Denby,
the good glasses chinking. Drink-and-drive laughter,
work talk, bridge bids: all the bafflements of adulthood.
Distantly we orbited something bright and brittle.

Nests of hangers have been wrestled into quiescence,
an astonishing number of binbags filled when,
beneath the suit-bags and orphaned boot trees
I'm startled to see pink-flesh plastic: our old dolls,
names long forgotten but lips still pursed for bottles,
the fringed eyes stiffly flapping. I shove mine
into a 'tip' bag but fish it out again later; intrigued,
uncomprehending. It takes a friend, another mother,
to decode this: *you were always her **little** girls, you see.*

from the dark side

Linda Burnett

it is *a shock*
- the obverse *perception*
of a howling moon that *carcass-jolting*
drama queen of monochrome *summoning the*
cliché to signpost lunacy in the dread *deadened cells*
of night wreaking havoc on unsuspecting folk *almost numb with*
their certainty clawed away by fear rather it's like *long hibernation*
seeping out of consciousness gradually impenetrable to *fingers of light*
prodding from uneasy sleep toward the dark side without *promised hope*
raising lids outside dissolves barely a thought of casting for *a lifeline that may*
help to clamber out of the quicksand watching the grain slide *turn the neap tide*
starting to swallow air struggle sucks you further down you gaze *at the new moon*
in space whittling about the lifespan of that black dog strangely *it feels like spring*
teasing absorption from yourself focus diverted from the inside *knitting together*
prepared to be woken and to engage again the hourglass tilts *unravelled threads*
dragging back the liquefaction of the bones sensing solidity *warmth suffuses*
ice thaws once more to expose new buds sleepers stretch *every weary bone*
in readiness for the next phase nights give ground *to leaven days*
till curtains can't contain the dawn they crack *with expectation*
rupturing a chrysalis of crumpled sheets *there is kindling*
time to reflect then rouse to wonder *at what's to come*
seize the day before it passes *deny the old*
darkness bearing down *embrace*
until full moon *the new*

Seducing Tom Jones at the Travelodge in Slough
Di Slaney

I must say as disclaimer, this never happened. But if it had, the
scuffedup lift doors would have closed with a clang, green
acrylic carpet sending static thrills all up my tights, green
capital letters saying PRESS HERE on the pad, the smell of grass
rising tangyhot around us—we'd found a quiet kissingpatch of
lawn behind the kitchens that reminded him of home—

the cuttings sticking to my skirt, his mind perhaps on home
and wife but his gorgeous brawny thighs pushing the
fabric, tracing the pattern, rubbing the swirly limegreen
flimsiness against my sweaty skin, burning chiligreen
with each bump and grind and still that stench of grass,
sweet and rich, filling the lift with the sticky scent of

June on a lawn in Slough, with the grumblerumble of
M4 traffic muffled by the lift, this metal box a new home
for weldingthighs, for however long it took to reach the
room, his or mine, the awful nylon carpet tracking green
up to the door, him on fire tighttucked behind me, mintgreen
breath cooltickling my ear, licking my mind like grassy

banks stroked to purring by the wind, not like the hotel grass
braziliancropped with patchy earth, the peep and swipe of
roomkey high and clear, us tumbling through the door as if home
was a Travelodge bedroom here in Slough, his hairy arms the
strongest grip, me up against the smeary window with its green
striped curtains we kept halfopen or halfclosed, that green

light flickering on the bed as his hands worked me over, my green
eyes open all the time, as greedy to take him in as sheep on new grass,
and if I didn't remember how the clothes came off, that trail of
trousersskirtbrapants a lazy S-shape to the bed, I knew that home

134

had vanished in the laughing tugandpull, the skinonskin, the
big raw taste of him filling my mouth with tart green

wanting. We lay a while afterwards—he said my eyes were so green
they'd called him from the café queue, that I was delilahgreen
with cunning and he liked that in a woman, loved the rub of grass
against my belly, his dark voice rolling so the choirsounds of
Wales bounced off the walls, beginning to draw him home
and fade me away. This never happened but if it had, the

afternoon would have ended greenslow, greenglowing
through our window from the grass below, those little flecks
of home refracted in the pale blue of his eyes.

Sous Les Étoiles
Harry Lowery

This city is a moonlit stave:
every balcony, terrace, and
belvedere reflects lamppost
light. The sapphire midnight
makes sheers and bedsheets
sway. Stars, the shade of
champagne, flicker in the
ballet of the dying sky, like
fireflies. Silent pavements
become sapient reservoirs of
skeletons…every death is a
Nocturne: Nabokov, Calvin,
Klee, Borges, Hesse, Nestlé
Erasmus, Joyce, Chanel…the
soundless streets are dark
sonnets hidden in the smoke
of cigarettes after the cinema
—those stars and these streets
play softer melodies than
violins: they alleviate despair
and astonish the hearts that
listen to every minim and
semibreve of the city.

Sweet Briar Plantation Burial Ground

Matt Hohner

Sweet Briar College, Amherst, Virginia
Juneteenth 2022

The sign reads, innocuous, carved and serifed font,
lichened and undersized in a small mown dell
of clay dirt the color of hemorrhage rubbed bare
by time on a slope facing a grove of hardwoods
and pines at the edge of awareness, no arrow pointing
the direction into a darkness history knows is there.
Skinned knee. Blistered hands. Flesh opened in daily
conversation with the overseer's angry and selective
God. Walk the path into the forest, into quiet stasis,
into a past of shadows. Come to a clearing thinned
of trees, rough and unkempt. An iron gate, rusted
and latched, stands fenceless, holding no one in,
keeping none out. The only way those here could
escape was into the ground. A rock with a bronze
plaque names them *founders* next to a sign showing
a map of numbers and ovals marking where they lay.
One could do the work, search the county archives
for ledgers of property bought and sold, learn their
names, make them more than chunks of quartz and
granite. But the rock reminds us that its makers bend
the past to suit the present, scrub the truth to rhyme
with words like convenience, expedience, closure,
erasure. In a lexicon sourced from the River Lethe,
mass grave becomes *monument*; *slaves* become
founders. Call them *more than sixty stones*, call them
more than a dozen unmarked burials indicated by
depressions in the Earth. Call them *families* versus
family groupings. Call them *mother, father, daughter,*
son. Call them. Nearby, a cardinal sings *Here! Here!*

Here! Here! as a late-day breeze choruses the green
canopy. Slant sun reaches its hands through the trees
into the soil holding ribcages and names to lift them up
into a future light for which they prayed and died, waiting.

When your Jamaican Grandmother Sings to you
Laura Ross

I listen with my eyes. Your new bones
attuning to an old song.
Your mouth rounding open.
You're already a choir, angel.
A myriad of assembled voices
wrapped in a baby-pink blanket.

Your grandmother's voice— a port city,
ballsy notes of venders, shucked scales,
thumping of boat hulls on a tallawah tide.
Wind in all its lush and leafy affirmations.

We river together,
                her and me
                      in you.

Our marrows, full of syllables
once shushed and braided beneath
the deft fingers of our tribal mothers.
Mine is a blueprint of winter light,
a palate of birch and wheat,
milky and spooned in.
Am I more visible in this white skin?
Our histories, a different kind of submission.
We are women, after all.

I want you to know I am listening,
that I am disquieted by your connection.
There's no lullaby in your grandmother's song
of safe keeping. You'll be judged and categorized,
little one, throwing your arms up now
as if they're feathered. Your voice, a wishbone,
an infant stage of mouthing textures, vowels
and consonants gathering and ringing out.

When I Was Anna Pavlova
Mary Mulholland

She took her company to the swannery
to see how they curved their necks, fluttered
wings, arched torsos in abandon. To an echo
of oboes, string tremolos, and harp arpeggios
the ballerinas waved arms in tender ripples,
seductively swayed, trembled feet. On points
Anna-Odette, arms folded was circling, dying.

When you took me to Abbotsbury, we stood
ankle-deep in feathers like a pre-coital pillow
fight, mute as the white bank around us.
We threw them food from buckets, took photos,
but were so far from dancing. I could spell
the song in swan as I watched them swim
out to sea, as if it were the Styx.

2022 CYGNATURE POETRY PRIZE
PRIZE WINNER

Cygnature Poetry Prize
Judge's Report
Cameron Stuart

Constructed from moments of easing and possibility, but also from crystallizations of restriction and separation, the last year's rampant fluctuations of being can be seen in the diverse spread of entries in this year's young poet offerings. There were a number of poems that sought to suffuse something magical, unexpected, and charged in their examination of familiar spaces and routines, looking into the domestic space and into the dislocation of normality that has characterized recent times, and producing some incredible responses to this. Equally, a number of poems sought to connect with other geographies, eras, and cultures, with a number of really excellent poems that turned to history and language as their sources of exploration, with some excellent uncovering of hidden histories, as well as using the past as a mirror to hold up alongside their own current predicaments. Moving through submissions was to climb in and out of narratives that stayed close to home, and into formal metered forays into the past, and also sensorially rich poems that looked to language, food, and music as portals of poetic exploration.

The quality of this year's submissions was really high, and it was thrilling to see such intelligent engagement with formal poetic structures, as well as a lot of experimentation with the balance between text and page space, and some fantastic experimental forms that often paid off and created nuanced and unexpected poetry.

In collating my thoughts on the entries this year as a cohort, I am reminded of Mary Ruefle's idea that 'we are all one question and the best answer seems to be love—a connection between things'. Interconnection feels at the heart of many of these poems: poems centre around loss and pain seem to understand and speak to the lack and loss of that rich connection, whereas poems of longing, desire, and faith, thrust their tendrils out to the world, asking for empathy, shared experience, or at least some partial translation or transmutation of values.

Whilst the deliberation around my eventual winner was tough, made pleasantly so by the strong contenders that joined this poem on my shortlists, I was most taken with this poem due to its mystery, intense empathy, and its ability to call on several modes at once, feeling tangible and tender at the same time as feeling wonderfully surreal, mythic, and open to interpretation. I am always attracted to poems that feel they wish to ask more questions than answer, and this poem does that in every line. The poem continues to work in these unexpected ways; there is a sense of what has been lost, and not carried, through to the presentness of this poem, but also a sense of what remains internally eternal to the speaker and the poem's landscape. The poem so deftly utilizes massive existential sized imagery alongside tactile micro details, and does so with such consistency in voice, so that the visceral moments 'dried blood' and 'throat knots' arrive alongside edges of 'absence', and staircases of 'names'.

One thing I don't wish to do in this brief preface to what I hope you'll agree is an incredible poem, is to try and lay out the narrative for you, or suggest how to 'feel', because I think one of the great successes of this poet is that these feel open to the intimacy of poem to reader. There are so many good lines here that I could just quote the whole poem in different order again and again in my spiel. There feels a connection with haiku and ghazal forms, with repetition and reconstruction of image, but I also often felt the poem reminded me of the richly emotive surrealism of poets like Pierre Reverdy and Joyce Mansour.

Turn the poem over in your hands and on your tongues several times. Savour it, then turn back to take another taste.

short cycle
Scott Lilley

"twenty dollars can buy many peanuts"— Homer's Brain, The
Simpsons, Season 5 Episode 8

In your right jean pocket, leather.

Stretching the bread we earn together, the leather of your arse
stretching the leather of the sofa, idle to axe your stomach's barrel to
curve over the sofa, our time peels away as sweat soaked faux leather.

Our time as constant as you, leathered from a Wednesday night,
imprinting the sofa, telling me you've disturbed language, spun grunts
into new dream, drank til the floor spins like a washing machine
underneath the leather of your jaundiced bare feet. You are here, so far
from any early golden season, alien so far from alien, yearning for
income, some spin for your yarn, peanuts for your wallet, your leather.

One of your episodes, fingers casting to coddle the nut of the nut
retrieve the deep savings from the sofa; money too tight for steak but
loose enough to spin to your desire. Commute, payroll, short cycle to
keep fit, through thirty-four seasons, cycle through the years. Money
too tight, the leather of your wallet in your jean pocket stuck in the spin
of the washing machine, worn resin to show for cheap leather. What to
show for the years on the sofa? Stupid poetic justice? You are losing
purpose, cycling through snoring motion, through politics spinning like
money laundering. You are Homer on untanned leather, Iliad on
yellowed parchment, and Homer stepping to leather, yellow eye, Mr
Burns. House sparrows flirting so far between hedges, nipping at the
feed to feed, this pin of routine, set reset, the cycle.

You had not thought and had undone so many, lead the masses, not the masses, lead the sofa, not the sofa, no, nothing to lead or be done, which has not been spun before, that which holds more, character, good, the cycle of what came before. This. Anything at all cromulent. No, there is no start greater than no start; no cromulence. House sparrows flirting between houses spar over the leather of day-old apple peel, fleeting, so quick, no long cycle. Cultural flit. *No, no, no, now shoo, shoo off the sofa*— the cat hair clogging the throw, the cat hair spinning the wool, the cat hair clogging day-old crumble. Spin as your younger self in the grave, carpe diem cromulent as seizing a ten-year old's neck, a life so constant so far from constant. *Yes, hiss, better you peel skin than leather, watch it watch it.* Lash out, lash out, there is no cycle without an expectation. *Homiee Homiee*, lost cycle of youth, your head of hair golden era. *Set to spin, no, no, we'll hang it, tissue it, hairdryer the leather to stop its sweat*— a swollen, perfectly uncromulent, water bulged wallet. Cheap leather, resin worn softer than sex. Bottom of the barrel leather washed, suffice to say nothing of culture lost. Nothing to break, cycle the years, this is culture significant, wide, cromulent. Your tenure up, our ten-year old's neck spinning in your hands, spinning, spinning to free his leather.

2022 BEDFORD POETRY
PRIZE WINNER

Bedford Poetry Prize Judge's Report
Liam Coles

This understated love poem has the gift of candour. It builds a beautiful edifice from simple materials, proving that it is difficult, yet possible, to write both simply and well. It refreshes a well-trodden theme, feelings of overwhelming love for another, by playing with cliches and cliched writing in a pleasing way. There is an excellent use of monosyllable throughout the poem; take the opening couplet:

> I want you to know
> that to me you are holy

The only disyllabic word is 'holy', the title of the poem, and it enters the line as a beautiful arrival. The speaker attempts to define how and why she feels as she does towards her inamorata; I was reminded of Elizabeth Barrett Browning's sonnet, *How Do I Love Thee, Let Me Count the Ways.* Small details are reified in the poem. The way her interlocutor 'catches' her bottom lip (I have not heard this word used in this way); how her eyes turn silver with tears—the silver representing the glistering rewards of the relationship. The feelings of love enable access to the numinous: she writes that *there are worlds within you*, in what is perhaps a paraphrase of Walt Whitman. The speaker turns to the mythological in the exquisite stanzas:

> Because when I touch
> Your skin I feel selkies
> Beneath the wash of the waves
>
> When I look into your eyes
> Rain falls on the sidhe from
> A pearl grey old world sky

'Selkies' and '*sidhe*' look almost out of place among the simple language of the poem, and this is, I think, the point. Here, love is an extraordinary passage in her life, akin to a religious experience, and that is why I think that the poem is called 'Holy'. Towards the poem's close, the word *linger* is isolated on its own line in a beautiful encapsulation of hopeful expectancy.

Holy

Lucia Wilde

I want you to know
that to me you are holy

The way you catch
your bottom lip
with your teeth

How your eyes turn silver
when they're full of tears

(I felt bad for noticing it
and loving it too)

(for falling *in love* with it
And with you, then,
In your tears)

It's that cliche
There are worlds within you
But it's true

Because when I touch
Your skin I feel selkies
Beneath the wash of the waves

When I look into your eyes
Rain falls on the *sídhe* from
A pearl grey old-world sky

On to the green, green grasses.

A year and a day they say
You've given me a year

And on the day I shall, wilfully,
(and fully knowing, fully wanting)
Eat those fruits and
Linger

With you.

Biographies

Juna Bine is a writer and visual artist based in New York. Her work includes sculpture, performance, video, and language-based work. She was a member of the first cohort of writing fellows at the Theoria Foundation, and her writing was selected as a finalist in the F(r)iction short story contest, judged by Madeline Miller. She is currently working on her first novel, *Run the Mountains, Run the Woods,* which deals with themes of ecosystem collapse, the afterlives of art in the wake of local human extinctions, and the limitations of community care when facing vast and powerful systems of injustice.

Linda Burnett, a Yorkshire-born former secondary school teacher of English and Special Needs now lives in Nottinghamshire. She won the 2020 Penfro Poetry Prize and the 2021 Walter Swan Poetry Prize and has had several poems published in anthologies and online. She has recently fulfilled a long-held ambition to complete an MA in Creative Writing at York St John University with distinction. She continues to write poetry with her local poetry group and to work on her latest novel.

David Butler, Irish author, had his second short story collection, *Fugitive*, published by Arlen House in 2021. Recent awards for the short story include the ChipLit Festival 2023, the Colm Toibin 2022 and the Benedict Kiely, 2021. His story, *The Rescue Dog,* made The Bedford Competition shortlist last year. He is also an award-winning poet, playwright and novelist. Dedalus Books is to publish his novel, *Jabberwock,* which he considers his magnum opus, later this year under the pen name, Dara Kavanagh.

Lucy Crispin is a former Poet Laureate of South Cumbria. She's published widely in print and online, most recently in *Channel, Poetry Birmingham, Pennine Platform* and *The York Literary Review.* In 2021

Lucy won the Ware Sonnet Prize and the Segora international poetry prize. Her pamphlets, *wish you were here* and *shades of blue* (both 2020), are available from Hedgehog Press or directly from the author. After a year out, she's currently working on her next, full-length collection, *hungers*, and has just won the Ware Sonnet Prize for 2023. Find out more at lucycrispin.com.

Claire Gleeson is from Dublin, Ireland, where she lives with her young family and works as a GP. Her stories have been published by The Ogham Stone, Lunate, Storgy and JMWW, who nominated, *We Are Approaching The Next Station,* for Best Small Fictions 2022. She is the winner of the 2021 Morning Coffee Writing Competition and runner-up in the Highlands & Islands Short Story Competition 2021. Her stories have been shortlisted for the Aesthetica Creative Writing Prize, the Anthology Magazine Short Story Competition and the Benedict Kiely Short Story Competition, and longlisted for the Bath Short Story Award, the Mslexia Short Story Competition and the Retreat West Short Story Prize. In 2021 she was awarded a Words Ireland literary mentorship. Claire's novel, *Show Me Where It Hurts,* was a runner-up in the Irish Writers' Centre Novel Fair 2023. She is currently seeking agent representation.

Anita Goodfellow has an MA in Creative Writing from Bath Spa University and a diploma in Creative Writing and Literature from the Open University. Her short stories and flash fiction have been placed or shortlisted in competitions and published in various anthologies. Her second novel, *So We Might As Well Dance*, is in its final stages. When she's not writing she runs a writing group and goes for long hikes. She tweets @nitagoodfellow.

Norman Goodwin resides in Seattle and Port Townsend, Washington. He holds a B.S. and D.D.S. degree from the University of Washington and an MFA from Warren Wilson College. His poems have appeared in numerous literary journals, most recently in *The Atlanta Review, Mudfish, TulipTree Review, Writer's Digest, San Diego Poetry Annual* and in a chapbook, *The Cost of Living* (Puddinghouse Press). He recently won a second place prize in the 2022 Writer's Digest poetry competition. He is currently writing a second chapbook and full length manuscript and has retired from the practice of dentistry.

Juliet Hill worked as a theatre musician in the UK for twenty years before moving to Madrid where she started to write. She has written a number of short stories including *Laughing Boy*, a prize-winner in the Writer's Forum magazine competition, *Property is The*ft, shortlisted in the Fiction Desk Newcomer Prize 2015 and a runner-up in the Storgy Magazine's 2015 short story competition, *Parka Billy*, shortlisted in the Highlands and Islands Short Story competition 2015, commended in the Southport Writer's Circle Short Story Competition 2016 and published in the Momaya Press Short Story Review 2020, *Onassis and Hoxha*, shortlisted in both the Writer's Forum Competition 2016 and the Bedford International Writing Competition 2020, *The Psychiatrist and the Cleaner,* highly commended in the Segora Short Story competition 2016 and shortlisted in the Earlyworks Press 2018 Competition, *Truth or Dare*, also shortlisted in the Earlyworks Press Competition, *Untroubled Waters*, 3rd prize-winner in the Southport Writer's Circle Short Story Competition 2020, *Bring it to the Yard Sale*, shortly to be published in the Canadian anthology *Not Without Us Too* and *Mavis Grind*, shortly to be published in the online magazine *Wishbone Words*.

Matt Hohner, a Baltimore native, holds an M.F.A. in Writing and Poetics from Naropa University in Boulder, Colorado. He is an assistant editor for poetry at *The Loch Raven Review*. Published in nine countries on five continents, Hohner's poetry has garnered numerous awards and recognition. He won second place in the *Connecticut River Review* 2021 Vivian Shipley Poetry Award and the 2021 Fish Poetry Prize, was shortlisted for the 2022 *Live Canon* International Poetry Competition in the UK, highly commended in the 2022 New Zealand Poetry Society International Poetry Competition and commended in the 2022 McLellan International Poetry Competition in Scotland. Hohner has also won the following poetry competitions: 2019 Doolin Writers' Weekend International Poetry Prize, the 2016 Oberon Prize for Poetry, the 2014

Maryland Writers' Association Poetry Prize (in which he also took third place), the 2015 Lascaux Prize in Poetry, and the 2018 Sport Literate, 'Anything But Baseball' poetry contest. His poems have been finalists for the *Cutthroat Magazine* 2020 Joy Harjo Poetry Award, the Sow's Ear Poetry Review Poetry Prize, the Cobalt Earl Weaver Prize for Baseball Writing, and the Moth International Poetry Prize in Ireland. He has been nominated for a Pushcart Prize and a Best of the Net Award. In addition to his awards and recognition, Hohner's work has appeared in numerous publications. Hohner has worked with artists in Baltimore and Maryland's Eastern Shore in two separate ekphrastic collaborations, and with Dutch composer Brechtje Vandijk (a.k.a. Bec Plexus), for a lyrical adaptation of his poem, *How to Unpack a Bomb Vest,* for her original musical composition inspired by the poem. His chapbook *States* was published by Third Ear Books in 1999, and his first full-length poetry collection, *Thresholds and Other Poems* (Apprentice House Press), was published in 2018. Hohner has held two residencies at the Virginia Center for the Creative Arts, and has a forthcoming residency at the Anam Cara Writers' Retreat in Ireland. A former public high school English teacher, Hohner has taught in-person poetry and creative writing workshops at the secondary and undergraduate levels, at Creative Alliance in Baltimore, and online with the Eastern Shore Writers Association in Maryland.

Andrew Kingston lives in Luton and works as a university administrator. He is a long-standing contributor to Clod Magazine and is part of the Luton Haiku project, which was included in the 2015 *Guinness Book of World Records* for having published 'the most haikus about one town.' Andrew blogs about his writing practice as the Wednesday Writer and about the pubs he visits as a member of the 'All the pubs we have ever visited, ever' team, as well as running the book stall on the regular Utter! Lutonia spoken word nights. Having recently completed a Creative Writing MA at the Open University, Andrew is looking to develop his longer form writing. Andrew is a lifelong Luton Town fan, adequate drummer—having played in Home Counties indie bands The Knockouts, Arndales and Thrilled Skinny—keen 'non-serious' cyclist and cat lover. His favourite colour is green and his favourite food, snacks.

Judy Koot is a multidisciplinary artist and teacher based in the Netherlands. She works as a writer, illustrator and musician, and teaches all three disciplines. Her diverse stories and poems for children and adults have been published in Dutch, Belgian and British magazines and anthologies, were longlisted and shortlisted, and won prizes, including the Dutch ELLE Poetry Award in 2002. In 2005, her children's picture book, *Het huis van Lotte Hanoeman* (The House of Lily Hanuman), was published by Belgian publisher De Eenhoorn.

G.R. Kramer grew up in Canada, Kenya and the U.S., the child of refugees from fascism and communism. He lives in the Washington D.C. area. He has written poetry for years for his own pleasure, and more recently for publication. At that he has been modestly successful after a lot of effort, with publication in several dozen journals including *Mudfish, Atlanta Review and New Verse News* and has been a finalist in many poetry contests including Writer's Digest, and Winter Anthology. Shortlisted in The Bedford Competition 2023 is of course the diamond in his crown. Kramer takes solace in Sylvia Plath's remark, "I love my rejection slips, they tell me that I'm trying". His first poetry chapbook, *Locomotive of Mangled Parts*, is forthcoming from Finishing Line Press in June 2023.

John Langan was born in Yorkshire in 1959 into an Irish family. His stories have been short-listed in several other competitions, including the Bridport Prize, Fish Publishing Short Story Contest, Frome Festival Short Story Competition and Kingston Short Story Prize. He has worked as a solicitor since 1984, mainly in London but with a period in Budapest. He now lives in Surrey.

Scott Lilley is living in the north-east working remotely as a communications and content coordinator at a facilities management company. Scott is also the communications coordinator at Osmosis Press, working closely with their weekly featured writing to promote new work. He began writing poetry as a cathartic practice before developing and growing via feedback and critique received at an after-school writers' group. Through this group he was able to perform his work at the Edinburgh Fringe Festival and Wenlock Poetry Festival. During this time, he was heavily influenced by performance-based poetry and enjoyed musicality, rhythm, tone, and repetition. Scott went on to pursue an English and Creative Writing undergraduate degree at Lancaster University and graduated with a First. He then enrolled in am MA in Creative Writing at Oxford University, achieving a Distinction on graduation. Through these studies, Scott developed a greater appreciation for poetry of the page and form. His final project for his MA was written under the supervision of Helen Mort exploring the limitations of the form of the sonnet and its historic ties with masculinity. His poetry is particularly influenced by the work of Dan Power, Sylee Gore, Wayne Holloway-Smith, Hannah Sullivan, Alice Oswald, Terrance Hayes, Crispin Best, and Harry Man. Scott has performed his poetry in Berlin, and read a collaboratively with Martin Kratz as part of The European Poetry Festival. His work has been anthologised in Black Bough's *Deeptime 2 Anthology*, The Broken Spine's *BOLD: An Anthology of Masculinity Themed Creative Writing*, and in *Virtual Oasis* from Trickhouse Press. His poetry has been published by *Butcher's Dog, Wet Grain, Osmosis, 3:AM,* and *The Babel Tower Notice Board* among others. His poem, *Howdy Partner,* won Young Poet Network's Pop Culture Challenge. His piece, *short cycle,* included in this anthology, plays on the form of the sestina, incorporating its repetition pattern to build into itself. In the near future, Scott would like to study towards a PhD, however his current main goals are to submit his work more frequently, read and workshop poetry more regularly, and to maintain a better work/home/life balance. Mostly, he just hopes people enjoy reading his work.

H. K. G. Lowery is a writer & musician from Gateshead, United Kingdom. He gained a Distinction in his MA in Creative Writing from Graduate College, Lancaster University, where he worked with Paul Muldoon, Paul Farley & Terry Eagleton. The Department of English Literature & Creative Writing awarded him with the 2021/2022 Portfolio Prize for his 'outstanding performance' as highest achiever in The Faculty of Arts and Social Sciences. Lowery has been shortlisted in The Bedford International Writing Competition and The Terry Kelly Poetry

Prize and long listed for The Fiction Factory Flash Competition. His publications include: *An Enquiry into the Delight of Existence and the Sublime* (Austin Macauley Publishers, 2020), *Being and Becoming* (Kindle Direct Publishing, 2021), *Death, And Other Angels* (Errant, 2022), *9:45 Drama* (Kindle Direct Publishing, 2022) & *Moonflowers* (Aurum Journal, 2023). To date, Lowery has been published in: *Poetry Salzburg, Amsterdam Quarterly, Pennine Platform, Obsessed With Pipework, Publishers Weekly, Hyacinth Review, The Ofi Press, Hearth & Coffin, StepAway Magazine, Dreich Magazine, Granny's Tea Poetry Magazine, Train River Publishing, Lit Shark Magazine, Sylvia Magazine, Patchwork, Wildfire Words, Lancaster Flash* & *Disabled Tales.*

Mary Mulholland is recently published in *Finished Creatures, Raceme, The Rialto, Aesthetica, Stand, Spelt,* and several anthologies. This year she's also been longlisted in the National Poetry Prize, Rialto Nature & Place, placed in Wolves, Teignmouth, shortlisted in The Bedford Competition, Fish and Plough, and commended in South Downs and Ver. She is completing her first collection and has a pamphlet, *What the sheep taught me* (Live Canon, 2022), plus two collaborations with Vasiliki Albedo and Simon Maddrell: *All About Our Mothers* and *All About Our Fathers* (Nine Pens, 2022/23). She founded the poetry platform, Red Door Poets, co-edits *The Alchemy Spoon*, and has a MA in Poetry from Newcastle University. Former psychotherapist and journalist, she lives in London but occasionally farm-sits a fine flock of Barbados Blackberry sheep.

Eve Naden, born in France, now lives in the UK where she studies English at the University of York. She writes everything from short stories to poems, screenplays and very long novels about very angry women. Passionate about her working-class roots, she wishes to one day tell the story of her ridiculous but wonderful family. Her work has featured in the Roadrunner Review, the Elmbridge Literary Magazine, and the Cheshire Literature Anthology. She likes to write worryingly honest stories about the difficulties of being a functional adult. At some point, she hopes to become a published novelist.

Damen O'Brien is a multi-award-winning Australian poet. Damen's prizes include the Moth Poetry Prize, the Peter Porter Poetry Prize, the New Millennium Poetry Prize and the Cafe Writers Poetry Competition. Damen's poems have been published in many journals including *New Ohio Review, Mississippi Review, Poetry Wales* and *Cordite*. Damen's first book of poetry, *Animals With Human Voices,* is available through Recent Work Press.

Jesse Perrin was born in Bedford and has lived in the town and its surrounding villages all his life. On leaving school at fifteen, he became an indentured apprentice bricklayer. He studied at Mander College for City & Guilds qualifications and became a part-time lecturer at the college, before going on to establish his own business and design and build his own house. He followed this with a long career in academia as a lecturer at Bedford College, progressing from bricklaying lecturer to become head of the building department and curriculum manager for all college crafts. During this time he gained am MA. Latterly Jesse spent ten years as contracts and estates manager for a London business, managing the maintenance of industrial estates. To fulfil a long-held ambition, on retirement Jesse began to write short stories, with little thought of their eventual publication. He joined Rothsay Education Centre in Bedford where he was encouraged to submit stories for publication in magazines. His stories have now appeared in county magazines covering Beds, Herts and Bucks. Scribble Magazine has also published his stories. His favourite venues for writing are any number of local cafes and burger bars, their constant buzz of activity and ample coffees ensuring that he stays mentally focused and fully alert. His ultimate ambition is to produce an anthology of the many stories he has written.

G.H. Plaag was born and raised in Boston and currently resides in New Orleans, where they are conducting research for a forthcoming novel. They hold an MFA in Creative Writing from Hollins University, where they also taught, and have been published by the Academy of American Poets, the Winter Anthology, and the Hyacinth Review, among others.

Jean Ann (J.A.) Pollard is an author/artist who was born and currently lives in Winslow, Maine (after a few exciting misadventures in Malta, Libya, Tunisia, Russia, Bermuda, the Bahamas, England, southern France and, oh yes, California!) Over the years, she has interviewed and written articles about people and the environment for many newspapers including *The Bermuda Sun* and *The Christian Science Monitor*), while several of her non-fiction books such as *Polluted Paradise* (which examined early pollution problems in the State of Maine), *The New Maine Cooking* (which extolled careful cooking with healthful ingredients), as well as *The Simply Grande Gardening Cookbook* with husband, hydrogeologist Dr. Peter Garrett (which added gardening expertise to good cooking). Two children's books, *The Ice Ladder,* and *Least Angel,* were also published, along with short stories, poetry, and non-fiction in literary journals including *Bibliophilos* and *The Lamp-Post*; in anthologies such as *Going Postal* and *Haunted New England*; and in national magazines from *Audubon* to *Family Circle*.

Diana Powell is writer of short fiction. She was born and brought up in Llanelli, South Wales, and studied English at Aberystwyth University. Having moved around for many years, being wife, mother, housewife, part-time this-and-that, she and her husband settled in Pembrokeshire, and she settled down to write except, of course, she had always written. Most of us, she says, have a creative impulse of some kind, but the form it takes is uncertain. For Diana, her love of books provided the key that led her to writing, making her want one of her own. So, she was thrilled when her novella, *Esther Bligh* was published in 2018, by Holland House Books. In 2020, her collection, *Trouble Crossing the Bridge*, was published. In the same year, she was runner-up in the Society of Authors ALCS Tom-Gallon Award, gained third prize in the TSS Cambridge competition, and featured in Best (British) Short Stories. Last year, she won the Bristol Short Story Prize. Her novella, *The Sisters of Cynvael*, (winner of the 2021 Cinnamon Press Literature Award) will be published next year. Her novel, *things found on the mountain,* is out now, published by Seren Books. This is the third time Diana has won a prize in The Bedford Competition—something she is very proud of.

Ricky Ray is a poet, essayist, and eco-mystic who lives with his wife and his old brown dog in the old green hills of the Hudson Valley. He was educated at Columbia University and Bennington College, and he lectures on poetry, animism, and integral ecology. He is the author of *Fealty* (Diode Editions, 2019), *Quiet, Grit, Glory* (Broken Sleep Books, 2020), and *The Sound of the Earth Singing to Herself* (Fly on the Wall Press, 2020), a finalist for The Laurel Prize.

Laura Sobbott Ross has worked as a teacher and a writing coach for Lake County Schools in Florida and was named Lake County's poet laureate. Her poems have been featured on *Verse Daily* and have appeared in *Meridian, 32 Poems, Blackbird, Main Street Rag, National Poetry Review*, and elsewhere. She was a finalist for the Art & Letters Poetry Prize and won the Southern Humanities Auburn Witness Poetry Prize. She is the author of two poetry chapbooks and three full-length poetry books.

David Shelley Jones started writing a few years ago when his children were grown up and his medical practice in Sydney well-established. He was encouraged by winning the Medical Journal of Australia MJ Dark National Short Story Competition in 2014 and the Bath Short Story Competition in 2018. He was a finalist in the 2021 London Independent Short Story Prize. Three previous stories have been shortlisted in The Bedford Competition. Before moving to creative writing, David's publications related to gynaecological surgery and obstetrics, so he is enjoying the latitude of fiction. A novel is in progress. While city-based, David likes to spend as much time as possible 'off grid' in his caravan on a bush block in southern New South Wales. He's also spent time working in outback towns and in the United Kingdom.

Di Slaney lives in an ancient farmhouse in Nottinghamshire UK where she runs livestock sanctuary, Manor Farm Charitable Trust and an independent publishing house, Candlestick Press. She was the winner of The Plough Poetry Prize 2022, Brittle Star 2014 and Four Corners 2015 poetry competitions. Her poems have been broadcast on Radio 4, published in *Poetry Wales, Popshot, Magma, The Rialto, The*

Interpreter's House, Brittle Star and *iamb*, and highly commended in the Forward Prize and Bridport Prize. She has been widely anthologised and her most recent win is the Slipstream Open Poetry Competition 2023. Her debut pamphlet, *Dad's Slideshow,* was published by Stonewood Press in 2015, with her first collection, *Reward for Winter,* published in 2016 and a second collection, *Herd Queen,* in 2020, both by Valley Press. She is poet in residence at Nottinghamshire Local History Association and a member of the Wonky Animals Poetry Collective.

M.B. Thomas began writing short stories during the pandemic, as a response to the restricted life we were all leading. He had never written fiction before. Four stories have now been short- or long-listed in national competitions. His stories vary in style, but he is drawn to the unreliable narrator, the flawed memory, the sense that all is not as it seems. *I Can't Hear You*, the story in this collection, is about how in the end we are our memories. It is entirely in direct speech, dispensing with the formality of 'he said, she saids'. The list of authors he admires is long— Margaret Atwood, Carol Shields, Graham Greene. Several have published celebrated short story collections—Paul Theroux, W. Somerset Maugham, Annie Proulx. One of his earliest literary heroes was Saki, the master of satirical stories over a century ago. He believes the perfect novella is Antonio Tabucchi's, *Pereira Maintains*. M.B. Thomas lives in Manchester, previously in Scotland and North Wales. He has worked in health and education. His stories draw on people he has met in these sectors: their hardships and dilemmas. He has travelled widely but has a special love for Italian culture, from Botticelli to Barolo. One day he may write a novel but at the moment his ambition is to find time for more short stories, to follow up all those fleeting ideas, to finish the many opening paragraphs on his laptop. The appeal of putting everything into just 2000 words is for now irresistible.

Lucia Wilde was born and educated in Bedford, finding a love of reading and then writing whilst in school. They also enjoyed involvement with theatre and music during this time before moving on to study English Literature and Drama at the University of Sussex in

Brighton. Although struggling with their mental health during their degree, they graduated and spent some time trying to work out what on earth to actually *do*. Whilst the answers haven't been forthcoming, they have since returned to Bedford and now work as the Deputy Manager of Oxfam Books & Music in Bedford town centre. So they're using that degree. Sometimes. They still read, and write, and attend the Read Poets society in the Eagle Bookshop at the start of every month. Inspiration comes from anywhere and everywhere. The poems read at the society, work, conversations, other books, games of *Dungeons & Dragons* or creating stories with friends online. They have never written to be published before, aside from a short story that won an internal competition at university. Mostly, they just write for their own pleasure, and find it a joy if that writing reaches others. There may still be volumes of adolescent poetry locked away on various computers that will never see the light of day, but if there are we'll never know.

The Bedford Competition 2023

Share your words with us and the world

We invite you to submit stories up to 3000 words
and poems up to 40 lines long

Prizes
1st £1500   2nd £300   3rd £200

Judges

Short Story – Tim Jarvis
Poetry – Kirsten Norrie
Cygnature Short Story Prize – 17-25 yrs. – J S Watts
Cygnature Poetry Prize – 17-25 yrs. – Sarah Davies
Bedford Short Story Prize – Paul Barnes
Bedford Poetry Prize – Liam Coles

The Bedford Competition is a non-profit group. All net proceeds this year
will go to The Ridgeway School for disabled children, International
Refugee Trust and BDCPS, a charity that helps people with cerebral palsy.

Competition opens 1st May and closes
31st October 2023

To enter visit our website:
www.bedfordwritingcompetition.co.uk

Ingram Content Group UK Ltd.
Milton Keynes UK
UKHW011950020723
424412UK00001B/12